PICTURES OF YOU

a gripping psychological suspense thriller

DIANE M DICKSON

Paperback published by The Book Folks

London, 2020

ISBN 978-1-913516-81-9

www.thebookfolks.com

For Paul and Lynne

Chapter 1

Mary glanced down at her watch. She was going to have to rush or miss the bus. She really didn't want to take the car into town. It was a pain navigating the one-way system and searching for parking – all of that; this was a day off, a day of leisure, well it should have been.

With only one bus an hour from the local stop the whole day was in danger of falling apart.

This was all because of the time spent preening in the hall mirror, dabbing with concealer, trying to disguise the wrinkles at the corners of her eyes and combing her light brown fringe forward to cover the hint of a line on her forehead. Laughter lines people called them, and it was true that when she smiled the wrinkles deepened. They certainly hadn't begun in laughter. Bill's illness had aged her, dragged her down, highlighted her hair with spun silver, and then at the end spit her out, transformed from the young woman that she could barely recall, into a middle-aged widow.

Bill had always told her she looked as young as the day they were married. Bill, who would now be forever young in the pictures on the mantelpiece. For a long time after he died, she had been mired in sadness, still though she didn't begrudge a moment of the grief. She loved him, lost him and mourned him. Now it was okay really. She coped well on her own and thought if he was watching from wherever, he would be proud and would wish her well.

She scurried around the corner and glanced backwards. There it was, the bus breasting the brow of the hill. Of course, today it had to be early. The stop was still a few hundred yards away, down the road. She quickened her pace. Typically, there wasn't much traffic, just when you needed a bit of a jam, a delivery truck blocking the inside lane or even a red light at the crossing, there was nothing and no one.

She broke into a run. She was going to miss it. No, no she bloody wasn't. She turned and glanced over her shoulder again and that was when everything went pear shaped. The pavement slipped from beneath her feet and there she was on hands and knees in the middle of the street.

She groaned.

"Hey, are you okay?"

She twisted her head. Looking down was a tall young man dressed in denims and a sweatshirt, blue eyes peering from behind a dark fringe.

"The bus!"

"Right!" He leapt away from her as she pushed to her feet and peered down at the dust on the knees of her navy trousers.

"Hey, no stop!" she called out.

He had reached the road edge, stepped over the kerb stones and was standing in the road waving at the grey vehicle. Of course it stopped, well how could it not? He had quite literally thrown himself in front of it. The brakes hissed and the motor juddered and complained at the rapid shift of gears.

Twin doors whacked open. The driver was visibly rattled.

"You bloody nutter, what the hell do you think you're playing at? I could have knocked you into the middle of next week. Shit!"

The boy turned back to Mary and, with an old-fashioned delicacy, took hold of her elbow and ushered her into the disapproving glare of the passengers and the driver of the number thirteen.

"Lady needed to catch the bus, man. She fell. Chill yeah."

Flicking a plastic wallet open to show his travel pass the youth then turned from the furious driver and leaned into the seat Mary had fallen onto. His breath was sweet in her face, his skin clear. He smelled faintly of some sort of deodorant or lotion.

"Do you have a pass or a ticket?" he asked.

She held out her own wallet and he waved it in the direction of the front of the bus.

"Are you okay?"

"Yes, yes, I think so. You shouldn't have done that, you know. You really shouldn't. If you had been hurt, well…"

His face split in a great grin and she couldn't help but smile back at him.

"Thank you erm…?"

"Jake."

"Thank you, Jake, it was silly and you shouldn't have done it but thank you."

"You're welcome, are you sure you're okay?"

"Yes, yes, I'm fine. I feel very silly but I'm fine."

With a nod of his head and a second beaming smile he turned from her and made his way to a seat further back. She felt shaken up, embarrassed and something else; she felt a little thrill. It was a nub, a tiny glowing bead somewhere deep inside and she couldn't have said what it meant but it was a feeling from the past, from the days of youth and excitement. She held it for a while for it warmed her soul.

Chapter 2

Mary closed the front door with a thud and then leaned against it for a moment before she took off her coat and draped it on the chair in the hall. She slipped out of her shoes, wiggled her toes and sighed. In the end it hadn't been a good day. The early sunshine faded and dull grey clouds leaked down onto the pavements and buildings. Lunch had been a disappointment but not in a way that could be identified, just – not quite right. There was nothing on her shopping list available in the colour, size, shape that she fancied. Jane had been irritable because her contact lenses were making her eyes sore and now it was just good to be home and she wished she hadn't bothered with the trip at all.

She threw the packets of salmon and vegetables onto the kitchen counter and poured a glass of white wine. Carrying her drink through to the living room she sank onto the sofa.

The little diamond in her engagement ring twinkled in the fading light. She lifted her hand and studied the jewel. She missed him, even though she had made a life without him, she missed Bill. This evening when everything seemed a bit empty and rather pointless, she missed his smile and the easy chatter that would have cheered the end of a frustrating day.

Roll on tomorrow, she thought. There would be company and work at the surgery to occupy her. Tonight, though, she felt unsettled; on edge. In the quiet, the little grain of memory that had been nibbling at the edges of her consciousness forced itself forward. She was haunted by his smile, his sparkling eyes. If they had ever had a son then she would have liked him to have had sparkling eyes… She gave herself over to the contemplation and a smile hovered at the corners of her own mouth.

She couldn't recall ever having seen him around before and yet, he had a pass for the bus, hadn't bought a ticket and so must be a regular traveller. She grinned to herself, and chuckled quietly under her breath. *Look at me, mooning over a boy. It's the shock I expect, the result of that fall. It's years since I fell over and when you get to my age you can't shrug those things off.*

She raised a finger to the tickle on her face, *what on earth?* Her cheeks were damp with tears. She had been totally unaware of shedding them and didn't know why she was crying. Tears for herself? But there was nothing to cry for. Tears of frustration for the wasted empty day? No that wasn't it? Tears because she fell? Well maybe – but she wasn't hurt. Tears for the past?

Maybe these were tears for the loss of passion and excitement. Tears of boredom, that's what they were, not just everyday nothing-to-do boredom, something more. They were in recognition of emotional boredom, an acknowledgement that she wasn't ready yet to be quiet, to let passion go, to be done with all of that. The fleeting touch on her arm, the smile, the smell of him, the closeness of a young male animal had stirred a desire that she believed had been lost, her skin flushed with the thought.

Perhaps she should consider looking for some male company, not online dating, nothing like that, but maybe she shouldn't be so sharp to dismiss the introductions of well-meaning friends. Dating, that was a scary thought, could she really do that? She shook her head. Let it go, just let it all go and calm down.

That was enough for one day, with no appetite for the salmon she tidied the food away and dragged herself upstairs. Sleep, that was the answer to all this introspection and soul searching.

Chapter 3

Rain fell for most of the night and the morning was dull. Water dripped and gurgled in the gutters. Mary stretched under the covers and was surprised to find her back stiff and sore. She swung her legs out of the bed and saw that her knees were bruised. She popped a couple of aspirins and creaked downstairs to eat a bowl of cereal. The garden was sodden, shrubs and trees flicked and twitched shrugging off the water. The poor weather did nothing to lift her mood, and the melancholy of the previous evening lingered. She sighed and hitched her shoulders. It was time to push this aside and get on with things. It was a long time since such sadness had visited and it mustn't be allowed to take a hold.

She backed the little blue Fiesta onto the road and turned towards the High Street. Why? Why do that? This wasn't the usual way. It was true that either way led to work, but by turning left she would avoid the bulk of the traffic and make the drive easier. Yet here she was turning the other way.

Silly, silly, the time was different, the day was different and the whole thing was ridiculous. Going this way on the off chance of seeing the boy again, hunting for Jacob. How stupid.

Of course he wasn't there. She turned her eyes towards the bus stop, flicked a glance up and down the road but the traffic and driving demanded her attention. Now she felt disappointed and ridiculous and tutted in irritation at herself. He was nothing to do with her, he was a ship that had passed in the night. What a foolish woman she was becoming.

The day improved and coming home from the surgery was pleasant, contentment had smoothed the edges of the day. Watery evening sunshine glinted on windows and the lowering sun painted pink streaks across the evening sky. Work had gone well, and she felt brighter.

Mary enjoyed her job. It was busy, and at times prickly patients took out their anxiety and fear on the receptionists, but she believed herself to be good at what she did. It was a good place to work and mostly, as now, she returned home satisfied.

She deliberately drove the quiet route, avoiding the busy main road on some fool's errand searching for the boy who had helped her. She tried to convince herself that all she had wanted was to thank him and that was the reason for the choice of route that morning. It wasn't true, and in her heart she knew that really what she wanted was to see him again, his bright eyes, that smile – it wouldn't do, it just wouldn't and that must be an end to it.

She cooked the food bought the day before, settled in the cosy lounge with her Kindle and pushed all thoughts aside of the fall and the brush with the boy. She would, however, think about her situation and look into joining an evening class or book club where she might meet someone who could fill this newly awakened desire for male company.

This young man, Jake, had done her a favour. He had made her look at the situation and realise she needed another layer to her life. There would surely be no harm in looking for some men friends. If the situation had been reversed, she wouldn't have wanted Bill to be alone.

Feeling happier she spent the evening with her novel and climbing the stairs to bed she believed she had wrapped the silly little encounter in common sense and tucked it away where it belonged, in her past.

Chapter 4

Two weeks went by with spring sunshine greeting many of the days. Mary studied the brochure for the local college and pretty much decided to take a class in photography. She had Bill's good camera and a "point and shoot" one of her own. When he died, friends suggested she take this route but at the time it had seemed to be simply a way to fill the huge hole left in her life and she hadn't wanted to fill it.

Though it was obvious life had to go on Mary had welcomed the pain. It was something to focus on, a sharp and powerful feeling of loss and anger which kept her from falling into the deep pit of depression and emptiness that had beckoned.

Even now, in moments of total honesty, she wasn't sure she really wanted to do this. However, the strange melancholy she had experienced recently, disturbed her. Anyway, wasn't it good to learn something new, to hone and improve a skill and - well it was the sort of thing men liked wasn't it? There would be men there and it would be safe to meet new people in a public place. She would enrol. In the meantime, life had swung back to its usual routine, work, home and the odd trip into town or to visit friends.

"Can you go on the front desk, Mary?" The reception supervisor stood in front of her, a clip board in the crook of her arm.

"Yeah, sure. Is Chrissie not well?"

"Dental appointment."

With a nod of thanks, the woman spun around and swept down the corridor. Mary gathered her bag and jacket and relocated to the main reception area. A dental appointment. In the days to come she would think back to this moment and wonder how such a mundane event could have released the storm that it did.

"Hello."

Mary raised her head. "Oh!"

"Hello, hey aren't you the bus lady?"

Jacob stood before her, his face a little flushed. He was holding a white card in his hand and leaning down to speak into the grill in the window. He was taller than she remembered, probably touching six feet, and today dressed in a black jacket with his brown hair hidden under a knitted hat. His eyes were a mixture of green and grey, a tiny scar above the right eyebrow recalled the wonderful words she had read a long time ago in a Thomas Hardy book. She couldn't now remember the whole thing but it was something about flaws and the effect of them on perfection. She dragged herself back into the moment.

"The bus lady." She gave a little huff of a laugh. "I suppose I am, yes."

She could feel the skin of her neck warming and took a calming breath.

"What can I do for you?"

Should she let him know she had remembered his name? No, no need to do that.

"It's Jacob isn't it?" Oh, it was out.

"Hey yeah, cool – you remembered."

"Well, you're my hero." Now she felt silly, why had she said that? "Anyway, Jacob. What can I do for you?"

"Oh, I need to be registered. The college insist. I've just moved in, near here and I have to y'know get a doctor. I'm not ill though, but they need a doctor for the forms n' stuff."

"Yes, yes of course. Have you filled the card in?" She pointed to the paper in his hand.

"Yeah, do I – just – leave it with you?"

"Yes, but I have to make an appointment for you. You have to pop in and see the doctor, just to have a chat."

"Really? I don't know about that. Well, not that I mind, it just seems, well a waste of time, a bit of a fuss. I only need, y'know, an address."

"I understand but it's just the way we do things. It won't take long?"

He sighed, a flick of impatience ran across his eyes and he dragged off the hat. His hair stood in startled peaks for a moment and then flopped down, covering his brow and falling to the top of his eyes. He tipped his head to one side the better to peer at her.

"Shall I take your form, make the appointment and then it's done?"

"Oh, if there's no other way. Yeah, go on then. Thanks."

He grinned now and swept a hand across his forehead flicking the shiny fringe back from his eyes.

"That's it then, next Wednesday. I've written it on here. It won't take long, and in the meantime if you need a doctor you can call us. We'll send for your records from your last practice."

She watched him duck out into the brightness of the midday. When he had gone, she stared for a moment at the empty doorway. Her thoughts tumbled and a strange buzz slithered along her nerve endings.

Fingers flicking expertly across the keyboard she entered Jacob's details. He had moved into a flat just a few streets away from her home. She registered his age – twenty-one – he looked younger, maybe eighteen, not much difference though a couple of years, a boy really. Still just a boy.

She put in the electronic request for his medical records, filled in the virtual documents and clicked to move on to the next screen.

Sparkling eyes, an open, ready grin. His hair, dark and shining. A young body, firm and slender. The computer didn't ask for these details. The computer didn't want to know how it felt when he grinned at her, how she had registered the bony wrists and long fingers, fine and strong and stained with ink or dye. The computer hadn't seen him and felt the pulse of his life.

Just a boy.

Chapter 5

"Chrissie, could I ask you a favour?"

"Yeah, sure what's up?"

"Oh nothing, I just wondered if you could swap a day with me this week."

"Oh, well yes, if I can – which day?"

"Well, I just wondered if I could do your Wednesday and you take Thursday."

"Oh, yes. I think that's okay. Are you going somewhere?"

"Ah, yeah I'm going to see a friend, she can't do Wednesday. Are you sure it's okay?"

"'Course it is. Have a good day."

"Thanks."

As she turned to leave Mary was swept with a maelstrom of emotion. Embarrassment was uppermost, though only she knew what she had just done. There was a nick of shame, she had lied to her colleague. There was fear, if anyone found out what she was up to… but would it matter? Really? There was also a buzz of excitement. She would see him. She probably wouldn't even speak to him. He would probably use the automatic check in. But she would see him.

Her body was suffused with heat as she stepped into the street and made her way to the car park. Her throat dried, this was nonsensical, ridiculous. Perhaps she was starting the menopause, was this mid-life madness? He was a boy, a beautiful one but a boy and she had no claim on him. He wasn't a part of her life nor she of his. They had spoken once, no, twice; he had held her arm, ushered her onto a bus like an old woman and then he had come to her reception desk like so many others and given her a smile – it was so little really.

Wednesday couldn't come quickly enough. She would see him again and she wanted to see him again.

The days ticked by as they would. Many times Mary was tempted to speak to Chrissie and tell her a change in plans meant she could now go back to the usual routine. She knew the sensible thing would be to do that, to step off this silly merry-go-round and walk the path of sense and maturity. Then she would remember his smile, the heat of his hand on her elbow and recall the glint in his eyes. She would feel her empty world more deeply and her quiet life more sharply, and she would shake away the voice that told her to stop this nonsense. She convinced herself all she wanted to do was to make sure he was okay, to ensure his visit to the surgery went smoothly. It was simply repaying a favour. He had helped her, now she would help him. She could try to keep his waiting time to a minimum and, if he needed it, do whatever was possible to reassure him that his visit was nothing but a tick on a form and a click on the computer. That they were obliged to make sure they were keeping to the rules and fulfilling their legal requirements.

On Wednesday morning she applied her understated make up. See, she wasn't making any special effort. There was no reason to take special care, she was simply going to work, just doing her job as well as possible. She tried to help all the patients and he was new to the area, on his own, and hadn't wanted the appointment, not really, and so this was just doing her job.

The morning dragged. She glanced at the door each time it swung inwards. His appointment was for eleven, the morning was going well, the appointments a little behind but when were they not?

The draught from the entrance drew her eyes to the light outside and there he was. He entered in the wake of an old man with a walker. He looked impatient, tried to squeeze past at one point but couldn't. He held the door though, so the invalid wasn't banged by the heavy wood and then he was in front of the desk. His skin was tinted pinkly by the chill breeze outside. A blue scarf wrapped around his neck reflected the colour of his eyes. He grinned at her.

"Hello Bus Lady. Here I am, what do I have to do now?"

"Hello Jacob. You can check in on the screen or I can log you in."

"Oh, no let's go with the virtual receptionist." He smiled and spun away to stand before the monitor and poke at the screen. When he had completed the simple procedure he turned his head, throwing an arm towards the electronic check in. "Ta da."

She smiled back at him and waved a thumbs up gesture.

"It's Mary by the way."

He couldn't hear her through the glass. She had known that, so why had she bothered to try to speak?

He walked back to the window.

"Sorry, did I do it wrong?"

"No, no. Oh I was just saying – my name – it's Mary." She felt a fluster of embarrassment now, her face burned. What a fool she was.

He leant to the grill and spoke quietly. "I didn't think it was 'Bus Lady' really." And with a little chuckle he turned away and found a seat. She pushed away from the desk.

"Mary, are you okay?"

"What – oh yeah, thanks Penny – bloody hot flush, can you cover for me a mo? Just need to get a breath of air."

"Yeah, off you go, you look like a beetroot. You should have a word with one of the medics, they can give you something for that."

No, no they can't, there is no prescription to cure stupidity!

Chapter 6

Mary slammed the door closed and tore off her coat, threw bag and keys onto the hall stand and pounded through to the kitchen. She poured a tall glassful of wine and gulped half of it back in one long swig.

"What a prat. What a total and complete idiot I am."

She was mortified. Each time she replayed the short encounter with Jacob, and she had done it repeatedly in the last few hours, it had seemed more and more ridiculous. Now running it on the video screen in her brain she witnessed herself reduced to a simpering idiot, preening and giggling like a schoolgirl. She hadn't done that, had she? Had she actually flirted with him– oh god? No, no she just told him her name, that was all. Come on, pull yourself together.

Of course the reason for her high state of disturbance wasn't really about the actions but rather what she had thought and felt.

"Right this is to stop now. Absolutely stupid. What on earth is the matter with you woman? Are you truly going to start mooning over young boys – really – at your age? Idiot!"

There, she felt better. Telling herself off out loud released some tension and unexpectedly a giggle started to burble up from deep in her belly. She chuckled at the silliness of it all, grabbed the wine glass and still grinning took herself through to the lounge.

Bill gazed at her from behind the silver frame on the mantelpiece and she raised her glass in a toast, "Oh Bill, what an idiot I am. I do hope that, wherever you are, you are having a good laugh and not shaking your head in despair. I don't know what got into me. I think it was the fall, you know. I just think it was the fall and then – well yes, he is rather lovely. It's been such a long time since I spoke to a new man – you know, a stranger and it caught me unprepared. I'm okay now though. All better. Thank heavens I've got the day off tomorrow. It'll give me a chance to calm down and get back on an even keel. Oh Bill, I do miss you."

She made herself a sandwich and poured another glass of wine, a smaller one this time, and followed it with two big glasses of water and by the time she settled to watch the television, she felt calm again.

As the thought struck her it was followed by a wave of sadness. Just for that short time, although yes, it had all been stupid, it had been a rather wonderful feeling of excitement. Waiting for him to arrive and then speaking to him. She hadn't known that buzz for years and years and it was sweet. Ah well, maybe the photography class would be a means of meeting someone more suitable.

Now it was time to push all this silliness away. Jacob, ah, sweet Jacob, was gone away back into his own young life probably never to be seen again and obviously he would never think of her, it was over.

If it hadn't been for the dream that would have been the end of it.

If he hadn't come to her in the deep of the night, with his smile and his beautiful hands and his strong young body. If he hadn't reminded her what it was to feel, to really feel like a woman again she would have let him go. But he did come and she was roused from sleep by the pulse deep inside, insistent and demanding, a warmth that she could not deny. So she was reawakened and knew that he had touched her soul and she didn't want to be free of him. She wanted more of him and there in the early blush of morning she was lost.

There had been times since she had been widowed when she had felt the lack of a physical relationship keenly. Bill had been still young and though the last year of his life had seen him weakened, up until then their sex life had been full and active. Yes, she missed it and had found solitary comfort when the need had become great.

Now, as she showered and wrapped herself in a robe, she wallowed in the total relaxation that can only come from sexual release. The dream was vivid in her mind, real and close. For the moment she didn't want to spoil it with denial and embarrassment and false modesty, but she replayed the scenes in her head and felt her body respond with flickers of pleasure.

Of course she had only seen Jacob in the daytime, wearing his jeans and tops but her sleeping mind had filled in the blanks and curled on the sofa with her coffee cup cradled in her clasped hands the memory of what his legs felt like laying atop hers, his arms around her and his full young lips on her mouth was as real as any that she could now recall of her married life.

Chapter 7

The sun was warm on Mary's back. She was doing the first weeding of the season and brushing and tidying the patio. It was pleasant to have her coffee outside to know that later she was going for a walk. It had been a clever trick to spend the first few hours in busy work, all pretence though. She was going to walk to his house and see where he lived.

Her tumble into infatuation had been incredibly rapid. Maybe if it hadn't been for the dream there would have been a chance of escape but now – it was too late. She didn't eat lunch but dragged a jacket on over jeans and a sweater. In her mind if there was no effort at preening then it was more innocent. She wasn't trying to attract him but was simply going to see where he lived. So why was she lost in the muddle of her mind? She shook her head and then strode out in the spring sunshine.

It wasn't far, ten minutes walk found her at the end of a road of Victorian villas. Most were converted into flats or cheap bed and breakfast places, but it wasn't a bad road. The gardens were mostly paved over but tidy and though mismatched curtains spoke of shared buildings it was a pleasant place. He was at number sixteen at the far end.

The Street Where You Live, she understood now the lyrics of the corny, old song. There was a chance that she might see him.

What would she do if she did? Wave perhaps, simply smile and carry on, stop and speak, she didn't know. She hoped she didn't meet him, hoped she did.

He wasn't there. Slowing her pace, she peered across the tarmacked front garden, past two small cars and into the porch. She wanted to walk across, to find the bell that would connect to his space but a woman with a dog was walking the other way and it was enough to dissuade her. At the street corner, where a left turn would lead her back to the High Street, she paused, glanced back over her shoulder. Should she turn, pass again? No, it was too ridiculous, madness heaped on insanity, so she walked away, disappointment dragging at her feet.

Her day was empty now. There was no further chance that she might see him, no further excuse to be where he might be. She went home and cleaned a cupboard, tackled the laundry and moved towards the night when maybe it would be possible to be alone with him, with the warm memory of the dream and the heat of her imagination in the empty bed.

She slid between the sheet and duvet and thumped the pillows into a shape that suited her. Now in the dark there was time to replay what she had done. What had happened to her peace and sanity? She wasn't a teen or even a young woman anymore but there was no denying she had a crush on this boy.

She remembered the days of flirting. The thrill of being noticed and the excitement of the touch of a hand or the brush of a glance. Then there was marriage. She had been faithful and, though the odd chance had come her way, she had never been tempted to stray. All the excitement had faded away and become contentment.

If her life had panned out the way it had supposed to, she and Bill would have sailed into old age together. Their passion would perhaps have faded slowly into a deep friendship. Maybe not, probably there were older couples who still cuddled and had active sex but she was never to know. Fate had robbed her of the chance to grow old with her husband and until now, until Jacob, acceptance had seemed the only option.

As sleep carried her away she hoped for another dream, another mystical encounter, another chance to be with him.

Chapter 8

There was no dream. Sleep was deep and peaceful, and waking was a disappointment. Mary tried to recapture the sensation of the previous morning but it was wholly gone. She took her shower and ate her breakfast and told herself that it was for the best after all. It was embarrassing to remember the fool's errand down a road of houses where there was no need to go, searching for a glimpse of a boy she had no claim to.

She cancelled the enrolment at the photography class. There had never been any real enthusiasm anyway and it had merely been a reaction to events. She went to work, took on an extra shift on the Saturday morning and called Jane to arrange a trip on her next day off in the week. She was Mary, Bill's widow, middle aged and perhaps a little boring.

It was over.

The weekend stretched before her with no plans save a trip to the garden centre and a video and ready meal on Saturday night. She ate well normally but now and again it was nice to feel a little rebellious and this was the extent of her rebellion. A mediocre meal made by unseen hands in a factory, miles away, warmed in the microwave and eaten on a tray on her lap while she watched a movie. She chose an old favourite seen originally at the cinema but now enjoyed in the warmth of home with no journey afterwards. It had been enough for several years now and it would be enough again.

She felt hollowed out, devoid, depressed and old, very old.

Monday was bright and sunny. Mary rang Jane. It was just an idea, perhaps they could have a meal, something, anything to make life less – grey.

"Hello Jane, I was wondering, do you fancy a drink this evening, after work? Sorry I'm ringing so early but if we are going to go, I'll leave the car at home, take the bus so I can have a glass of wine… What, no, no I'm fine – it's been a boring weekend and I just thought it'd be a change. You will, great, smashing. I'll see you outside your office at half five. Brilliant. Thanks mate."

She dragged the door closed and turned her face to the sunshine. All was well, of course it was. The bus was due in five minutes, plenty of time, no risk of a dash and fall. She shook her head and her lip curled in a smile. Life was odd at times.

There were two people already at the stop. One of them a commuter she had met before, the other an old man with ragged trousers and a grey, wrinkled face. She smiled at them both and took her place in the line while glancing at her watch. Two minutes.

The hulking vehicle drew into the stop, the brakes hissed and the door thumped back against the bodywork. They always seemed just a little too vigorous and she wondered if they couldn't fix them.

There was a seat two rows back from the entrance, on the side behind the driver. She turned her face to the window as the big engine was thrown into gear and the bus drew away.

She felt the presence beside her. She turned and looked down, denim and white trainers.

"Hello again, Bus Lady."

Mary raised her eyes.

"Oh, hello. Hi, Jacob."

"Hello – erm, Mary."

He hesitated for a moment before using her name. Had he forgotten who she was? Did he think it was too familiar?

Now that the original contact was made, they were both unsure how to continue. He smiled at her and then glanced down, fiddled with his back-pack, and glanced at her again out of the corner of his eye.

"So, how are you?" She would be mature. She would handle this.

"Yeah, good. Do you catch the bus every day? Only I haven't seen you before, you know since the first day."

"No, today I'm going out, I might have a drink so…" She shrugged.

"Ah, right. You've got a car then. Is it your husband's? Well not your husband's but you know – well, shared I guess."

"No, no it's mine. But I don't always use it."

"Right." The silence between them was uncomfortable, Jacob glanced around no doubt hoping to spot a friend, an excuse to move from this place beside her.

"You off to college then?" She pointed to his backpack slouched on the floor at his feet.

"Yes, a bit late today but it's okay."

"What are you studying?"

"Media studies, photography, film making."

"Oh, I'm doing a course on photography. Well, no I'm not – not yet, I'm going to. Actually, no I was going to, but I changed my mind." She was gabbling, filling the air with junk.

"Ah right."

He wasn't interested, was he? She was of no importance to him, why would he care what she was doing, or even more what she wasn't doing?

"I prefer the video work really, but of course you have to have a knowledge of it all, I guess."

"Yes, it sounds fun."

What a stupid thing to say, she was speaking to him as she would to a child.

"Well, yeah. So, you're not going to do it then – your course?"

"No, no I don't think so. I was just looking around for a new interest, you know, something to keep the old brain ticking over."

"Oh, I shouldn't think you need to do that, though, do you? I mean you have a job and everything."

"Well yes, but it's good isn't it, to have other things?"

"Hmm, what does your husband do?"

"I don't have a husband. Not anymore."

"Ah." He nodded. Of course he would assume that she was divorced. She knew that it was often the case when people heard she was single. It didn't matter, he wouldn't care.

"He died."

"Huh?"

"Bill, my husband – he's dead. I mean I'm a widow, not divorced. I expect you thought I was divorced."

"Oh god, I'm sorry – about your husband I mean."

She tipped her head slightly. "It's okay, it's a few years now, since he died. I miss him but it's okay."

He had turned to her now, swivelling slightly in the seat the better to look into her face.

"It's funny, well not funny but you know, Widow, it's an old word isn't it? I guess it shouldn't be but when you say it you naturally think of an old person."

Mary glanced out of the window, embarrassed, unsure of his meaning.

"Shit, I didn't mean. Oh, I said that wrong. What I meant was, you seem young, you know – young to be a widow. Oh, shut up, Jake, you're just making it worse."

He threw his hands up in surrender and her heart thudded with sympathy for his awkwardness. She reached out and laid a hand on his arm.

"It's okay, Jacob, I know what you mean. Do you like Jacob or prefer Jake?"

"I don't really mind, though I do like the way that you say Jacob. Most people just call me Jake and you make it sound a bit special. Yes, call me Jacob – I like it."

Her whole body was warm, her spirit felt light, she wanted to reach over and touch his face. She breathed in the scent of soap and the background of lotion or aftershave that she had detected the first time. "You smell nice." Oh God had she said that out loud? She cringed.

"Thanks." He had gathered up the straps of his bag. "This is me. I'm going to the café before lectures – for breakfast! Hey, it's been nice seeing you."

Mary nodded her head.

"Maybe I'll see you again."

"Yeah. Although I am probably moving. This place I'm at – it's temporary. Some friends of my mum own it but it's already rented from next month. I'm looking for somewhere else. I guess I'll have to come in won't I, to where you work, when I get a new place – the address and all that?"

"I have a room."

It was out before she knew it was a thought and when it was too late to capture the words and hide them away.

"Really. Hey, do you let rooms then?"

"Well, no but you know, if you were stuck. I have a spare room. Anyway, look, if you can't find anywhere you know where I work."

Oh, what had she done? Please don't let him take her up on it, please, please.

As if he sensed her back-step he just bent and pulled his bag up from the floor and then unfolding his long legs he stood and stepped away from the shared seat.

"Thanks Bus Lady, I'll get back to you."

No, no don't oh God – please don't.

She felt her palms damp with sweat and a cold chill swept her body. What had she done?

Chapter 9

"Are you okay Mary? Really, you seem – worried, distracted – something."

"Yes, I'm fine. I've had a funny couple of weeks, my nerves have been a bit – on edge. That's why I thought it might be a good idea to have a night out. Can you come for something to eat, is that okay? Just something quick."

"Yeah, let's go to the Italian, the one up at the top by the church and you can tell me what's on your mind. I've known you long enough to be able to tell when you're bothered about something. Come on, finish your wine and we'll go and eat things with garlic."

They stood in the entrance to the restaurant, peering around for someone to seat them.

"I like this place," Jane said. "I wonder if that young waiter'll be here. You know, the one who was flirting with you the last time we came."

"He was not."

"He certainly was, and what's more you were twinkling back at him."

"Oh, I didn't."

But the memory made Mary grin. The young Italian had indeed been attentive and flirty. Though they had both known it was to ensure a decent tip, she and Jane, who had been divorced for two years now, had enjoyed the flattery and the attention.

They were seated in a dim corner. The smells of tomato and garlic made their mouths water and they ordered a bottle of wine. Her shoulders relaxed and as the tension drained away her mood lifted. She raised her glass.

"Here's to us. I am lucky having a friend like you, Jane. Thanks."

"Cheers, and don't be so silly, you've been there for me as well. When it all went wrong, with Stefan and me. Anyway, let's have it. What's the matter?"

"No, nothing. Like I said, I've just been a bit jittery. I suppose it could be – you know *my age*," she grimaced.

"Yeah, I suppose that's coming isn't it? You know you can talk to me though don't you, if you have something on your mind?"

"Yes, thank you. Oh, here we go, oh blimey, the staff has changed. Have we come on pensioner's night?"

They both stifled bursts of laughter as a geriatric waiter who had squeezed his drooping body into the restaurant uniform of tight black pants, red shirt and black waistcoat stepped up to the table. The uniform left bulges and ridges which rippled and poked as he brandished the menus and presented the basket of bread rolls. They controlled their giggles but by the time he left with their orders both women had watering eyes and could barely hold back the laughter. Mary felt so much better than she had for weeks.

"Jane, do you ever get lonely? Since you split with Stefan?"

"No, not really. Millie is still around a lot you know. She comes back from Uni about every other weekend, usually with a bag of washing and a mate. Then there's Alan, I'm still seeing him a bit. Why, is that what's the matter love?"

"No, no, well I didn't think so. I quite like being on my own a lot of the time, pleasing myself, you know, and I do have work and so on. No, I just wondered. Have you ever considered sharing your house? Mind you, I don't suppose you can with Millie still needing her room and so on."

"Christ no, how would you do that? I mean how would you know who you were sharing with? No – why have you – thought about it I mean?"

"Not really. I just wondered, how you'd do it, you know, what would be involved. Not that I'm going to or anything I was just wondering. Here, let me pour the wine."

Chapter 10

Of course she knew he wouldn't get back to her. It was one of those silly spur of the moment comments that everyone ignored. It was hard though, given her mood, not to imagine what it would be like having a man in the place. Male stuff in the bathroom and someone else sleeping in the spare bed. She would probably hate it, now that she was independent and used to having the space to herself. To share, especially to share with a young man, well not such a good idea really – anyway it wasn't going to happen. Thank heavens, she told herself.

"Phone for you Mary."

"Thanks, who is it?"

"Somebody called Jake, says he's a patient."

Her throat dried. *No, no don't let this happen, please don't let this happen.*

"Hello, Mary here, can I help you?"

"Hi, is that you Bus Lady?"

"Ah, hello Jacob, how are you?"

"Yeah, fine thanks. Listen, last week, when I saw you on the bus. D'you remember?"

"Yes, yes I do."

"Well we talked about my place, you know." Her nails dug into the palms of her hand, she had to swivel the chair around to face the corner for she knew that she was looking flummoxed and felt – guilty.

"Oh right, I do remember yes."

"Well, thing is I have found a new place."

She exhaled noisily, relief flooding her with weakness.

"Ah, good, that's good – I hope it's nice."

"Yeah, well I think it will be, a shared house but my room is pretty big and it's clean and handy for college."

"Excellent, so you want to give me your new address – yes?"

"Yeah, yeah I can do – there is something else though. Before I start, I want to say that you can say 'no' really and truly and I'll understand so don't worry."

"Okay, well what is it? What do you want to ask?"

"The room won't be available until the middle of next month and my flat, the one I'm in at the moment is let from the end of this month. Anyway, the thing is it leaves me with a couple of weeks adrift. Listen – I know it's a bit of a cheek but well, I just wondered, you did say you had a spare room..."

She couldn't speak, the silence stretched and grew.

"Look forget it yeah, I've got a nerve I know, I shouldn't have asked. Now I've put you on the spot. I'm sorry yeah. Forget it Mary."

"No, no Jacob, wait. I'm sorry, it's busy here and a bit noisy, of course it's fine. Yes, I wouldn't have said it if I hadn't meant it. When would you want to come?"

"Really, are you sure? Oh, that's brilliant, I can't afford a hotel and my only other option was Dave's settee. Are you sure Mary – really?"

She laughed warmly. How sweet he was.

"Of course I'm sure. Now when will you come?"

"Starting from the twentieth if that's okay, and we must agree some rent, right from the start. House rules and so on."

"Yes, you're right. I'll tell you what why, don't you come round this evening, have a look at the room and we can sort everything out."

"Brilliant – erm."

"Is something wrong?"

"Ha, well I don't know your address."

"Oh of course, have you got a pen?"

Chapter 11

Should she offer him tea and cake, or a beer? Maybe nothing, perhaps she ought to keep it casual but business-like. Just show him the room, agree rent and terms and then let him go. No, she couldn't do that, he would expect a cup of coffee at least.

There were biscuits and she would offer him tea but not make it until after he arrived, no prepared tray, no sugar bowls and plates of chocolate Hob Nobs. No, she must make it look relaxed, as though she was taking it all in her stride. Maybe she could appear as though this was quite usual for her, as though she let the room often.

Six o'clock, he was coming in an hour. She stepped into the shower, she wasn't preparing she was simply taking a shower earlier than normal, no point cleaning the bathroom and then splashing it all up again. Would he notice, did men – boys – notice things like that? Bill had occasionally wiped around the tub but she was never convinced that he would have known whether the room had been cleaned. She had already tidied around the kitchen. He had mentioned that his new place was clean so maybe he did care.

So many thoughts, spiralling and swirling. What was she doing? What the hell was she thinking? She knew nothing about this boy. Yes, he had helped her up when she fell and many people would have just walked by, but apart from that she knew nothing.

Perfume, no perfume? She usually had a spray so why not? As she wiped steam from the mirror she peered through the warm fog at her face. She looked flushed – yes well, she had just been in the hot shower. Her eyes sparkled – yes well, it was the moisture in the little room. She had butterflies in her tummy – yes well, that was because she was a stupid, stupid woman who was allowing herself to get into a flap.

She took a deep breath and swept through to her bedroom and pulled on the jeans and sweater. The full-length mirror called to her, she ignored it. She wouldn't preen, she wouldn't even look. It didn't matter how she looked. He was coming to meet his landlady and it didn't matter how she looked.

The doorbell sounded.

There he stood. He had his backpack with him and looked rumpled, he must have come straight from college. There was an end of day scent to him. He didn't speak but just grinned at her. She stepped back and swept a hand in front of her, indicating that he should come in. He dropped the heavy bag onto the carpet at the bottom of the stairs and glanced around. Mary pointed down the hallway to the bright kitchen.

"Do you want a cup of coffee?"

"Do you have tea?"

"Of course, come on. We'll sit in the kitchen if that's okay?"

He led the way glancing into the lounge as they walked through the hallway.

"It's nice, your house – it's very nice. Homely and warm. My flat's a bit shabby and I have trouble making it feel cosy. I miss that. My mum's place is lovely, like this –

a proper home. I know that's not very cool but – well it's true. She's a bit fussy, now and then you know, likes things 'tidy'". He made a little flicking signs with his fingers, placing the words in quotes.

He had dragged out one of the wooden chairs and now sat with his arms across the table. Mary filled the kettle and pulled the biscuit tin from the cupboard. She threw a couple of bags into the mugs and smiled at him as she stepped across between the table and the fridge. Suddenly her traitorous mouth ignored all her earlier musings.

"Have you eaten, Jacob? Have you had your dinner?"

"What – erm well no. I came straight from the Student Union. I'm going to have something when I get home."

"Do you want to eat with me? I mean we can just have something simple, I can make some omelettes, perhaps some salad – oh or maybe you like chips?"

He laughed.

"That'd be great but are you sure? I mean it wasn't what I was expecting."

"Well I have to eat and if you're happy to have something quick we can talk about the room and so on. Do you want to?"

Say yes, please say yes, stay with me for a little while.

"Great, that'd be great. Tell you what though, why don't I go to the off licence, down on the main road and buy a bottle of wine – I can't afford a posh one but..." he shrugged.

"No, you don't need to do that. I've got a bottle of white in the fridge if that's okay, or beer – I have some lager?"

"Oh excellent, would that be okay? Hey this is great." He leaned back on the chair and his shoulders slumped slightly. It was only then that she realised how tense he had been. She wanted to reach out and brush the hair from his eyes, she wanted to touch his skin.

Chapter 12

The spare room was a good size. It had a double bed and one wall was lined with wardrobes. The window overlooked the rear garden. It had been underused. She and Bill had visitors often but most of their friends lived locally, so apart from one or two business colleagues looking for a bed after a late meeting, it had remained unoccupied. Jacob was thrilled with it especially when she told him that he was welcome to store all of his things in the cupboards.

She had cleared out and reduced after Bill, and now there was plenty of spare storage. For a moment it occurred to her that the empty cupboards were a reflection of the way that her life had become – vacant and pared down.

They went back to the kitchen. Jacob had his beer, Mary poured herself a glass of wine and put together a salad and made mushroom and cheese omelettes for them. It was pleasant to have someone to chat to as she bustled around the kitchen. They were easy with each other. She didn't know what it felt like to be a mother, but she didn't think it was this. This was a thrill, she wanted him to look at her as a woman, not as an older woman, not as a mother but just as a woman.

"That was great, Mary. Thanks."

"You're welcome. I suppose we need to have a talk about how we are going to do things. Are you sure the room is okay?"

"It's better than okay, it's great."

"Well, you must use the rest of the house of course. I don't expect you to just stay in the one room. I'd like you to feel as though you live here, properly, you know. As though you're at home."

It was sudden, he stood and threw his arms around her, then he leaned and gave her a peck on the cheek. She laughed, from surprise and delight.

"You are lovely. A lovely lady. You really are." He stepped away. "We need to talk about rent don't we and food and so on?"

"Well, what are you paying when you share at the other house? Why not pay me the same as that and then for food, I'll just buy what I normally do, you get anything extra that you want and we'll sort it out as we go. Most of the time it's cheaper to buy for two rather than one anyway."

A glimmer of doubt showed in his eyes. "I don't want you to, you know, feed me – I can pay my way."

"Oh yes, of course." A warning bell told her she was going too far. "Of course, I don't expect you'll eat here every night, anyway. Will you? Well you can of course but – I don't really think, for a couple of weeks, you want to buy in a lot of food so, you know, let's just see how it goes on."

"Okay. Yes, that's good. Let's take it as it comes, yeah. Look I need to be getting off. I have a pile of work to do before the end of the week. Thanks so much, Mary, for the dinner and everything. Thanks."

She waved as he turned the corner of the road and then pushed the door closed. She hugged herself. What a nice evening.

She had the address of his parents in her hand. He had insisted she take it so that she could speak to them and they could vouch for him. She wouldn't do it. It was enough that he had offered. It was only a couple of weeks, there was no real need to tell anyone, was there?

Then again, she must be sensible, or at least try to. She lifted the phone and dialled without a clear idea of what she would say but the number was unobtainable so obviously she had misdialled. She replaced the receiver.

Chapter 13

"You don't have much stuff. Is this all of it?"

"Yes, that's the lot. To be honest I was worried you might think there was too much clutter. You know, with my camera gear and so on."

"No, no it's fine. Do you want me to help you take it upstairs?"

"God no, don't you dare." He threw his arm around her shoulders. "Thanks for this, Mary. I know it was a bit of a cheek and you took a risk but thanks for – well, being open to it, you know."

"Hey, you scraped me up from the pavement. You dived in front of a bus for me, why wouldn't I be 'open to it'?"

He squeezed her to him, side by side, she felt the boniness of his hip and the strength of his arms. She didn't know what to do with her own hands, felt embarrassed by the spontaneous closeness. Her arms hung stiffly at her side, awkwardly caught between their bodies.

Letting go he bent to pick up some of the boxes and bags of stuff he had brought round from his flat. There were pieces of kitchen equipment poking from the top. Mary could see bedding and other reminders that this was to be short lived, a hiatus, and then he would move on. She tried to block the thought, *just enjoy the next couple of weeks*, she told herself. *You'll probably be glad to have your place back by the time he goes*, but already the thought of the house empty was a chill wind from the future.

A meal was waiting in the kitchen, lasagne and salad, wine and dessert; it was a bit special, a welcome. Her instinct had been for candles but in the end she had set the meal on the round kitchen table and was glad, it looked friendly and relaxed.

They ate and chatted, one or two awkward silences tensed the air, but Mary felt that it went well, all things considered.

"Do you want to go into the lounge? I'll bring some coffee through. Unless you have something to do?"

"No, that would be lovely, this has all been a bit special. Thanks."

She smiled at him and pushed her chair away from the table. Yes, it had been special. She had watched the play of light in his eyes, the way his hair flopped when he moved his head and the flick and stretch of his long fingers as he made a point or reached for the bread. She had loved it.

They chatted for an hour and then he went to tidy away some of his things. Mary curled in the corner of the sofa with a small brandy, a perfect finish for the nearest thing to a dinner party since Bill had become ill. All those years ago now, all those months when she could have done this but hadn't felt the urge and eventually had lost the knack or the taste for it.

She heard him thumping about upstairs, the slide of the cupboard doors and the flush of the toilet in the tiny en suite bathroom. It was strange and exciting and she found her nerves were zinging with it all.

"I think I'll turn in now Mary." He called down the stairs and she walked through into the hall and peered up at him.

"Okay, in the morning, just do your own thing, you know, help yourself. There's cereal, bread, jam and so on in the fridge. Just root around until you find what you need. I leave quite early so I'll probably be gone before you. Well, I mean that day on the bus I was later than normal."

"Okay, I'll probably see you tomorrow then."

"Oh wait." She reached out to the hall stand and held up a little ring.

"A key, for the front door. I had this cut for you. I'll leave it here on the bowl."

"Great. Brilliant – thanks Mary. Goodnight."

"Goodnight Jacob."

Chapter 14

She should have told Jane, should really have told her family but now didn't have the right words. The moment to confide had been in the restaurant but fear of disapproval had stayed her tongue and now there would be offence. In truth the idea had been a tiny seed at that point and really could have come to nothing, well couldn't it? Now his being there felt like a secret and a little tarnished because of that. It would appear odd to mention it, as if there had been subterfuge and truthfully, she couldn't say that there hadn't been.

She fretted about it a bit, ran it through her mind trying to see it the way others would. Surely they would understand it was innocent. He was a boy, a person who needed a bed. She had a spare room, it was simple. The bare and honest truth on the other hand though was the roiling mess of emotions, the thrill at the thought of him coming home, the buzz when she heard him knocking about in the kitchen. The new warmth in the house as she lay in her bed with him just yards away on the other side of the wall, in the dark, muttering occasionally in his sleep. The mush of feeling confused and troubled her and yet these dark pangs were diminished by the pleasure of having him there.

She would walk into the lounge to find one of his books lying on the table or pushed aside on the floor and would run her fingers across the paper smiling at the distant contact.

When he had moved on that was the time to tell Jane. She would mention it to her family, casually so as not to hide the facts from the people who cared for her. Later, when the bathroom didn't hold the echo of him in fragrant steam. She would tell them he was a friend for indeed it was what he had become.

They were easy with each other. He knew how she liked her tea and about the little obsession regarding the order of sharp knives in the block. She put toast in the machine in the mornings when she heard him thumping around upstairs so it was ready when he appeared, still bemused from sleep. She soon came to see he needed to be quiet for a while until after the first cup of coffee and so they would sit in the neat little kitchen with the radio soothing the silence. Many evenings they ate together and as he told her about the other students and his studies, she felt her life unfolding though only now was it clear just how closed down it had all become. He brought a wider world into the house and peopled it with characters she would probably never meet and he made her laugh. He showed her his work and asked for an opinion as though it really mattered.

"There's an exhibition at the college next week, do you want to come?"

"Oh, yes that would be great."

"Tuesday, you don't need a ticket or anything. If you come to the exhibition space and let them know at the door, I can come and meet you. I have to be there to set up my stuff."

Later a chill of apprehension made her worry. She wanted to go but how would it be? How would he refer to her, would he call her a family friend? Then again perhaps it wasn't like that anymore. It had been so long since she had been with students, in that sort of an environment and she didn't remember. Did they bother with all that or would she simply be another body? She was shy about meeting his college friends and in the end said she couldn't come because she was meeting Jane. He seemed disappointed and she felt a loss. The chance she might have had to move into his life a little more, had been forfeited.

The days were flying and there was less than a week before the date he had given for moving out. She counted them on the calendar. The house would be hers again, solely. Already the fact caused a quiver of grief. He mustn't know, it wasn't fair to burden him with any sort of responsibility or blame. It was essential though to find a way to make sure he didn't disappear completely from her life. Surely that would be okay, to make sure they stayed in touch?

Chapter 15

"We should do something special."

Mary didn't raise her eyes. They were sitting at the breakfast table. The next day Jacob was moving out, already some of his boxes had been transferred to the new address. She waited for him to speak.

"Special?"

"Yes, before you go. We should do something, shall I make us a meal, a special meal I mean?"

"Well, would you rather go out?"

She had never considered it. They hadn't been anywhere together and the idea pulled her up short.

"Oh, I don't know – I hadn't thought about going out. I just meant a meal, some wine here, but if you think that would be nice…"

"Yes we should, my treat. You've been so great – it could be my thank you."

"Oh, you don't need to do that, you've given me rent after all."

"Yes, but I know it hasn't been enough, not really. I don't think it will have covered the costs, water, the heating and I've eaten your grub."

"But you bought some."

"Not much and you've cooked, loads of times. No, let me. I can't afford really posh, but let me. What about the Italian place, by the church?"

"No, no, not there." Why, why had she automatically discounted one of her favourite places, a place where many of her friends and colleagues ate? She knew, of course she did, but couldn't examine the motive, knowing she might not like what she found.

"No, let's do Chinese, you like Chinese?"

"Oh yeah, Chinese is good. The Blue Tower is supposed to be okay."

"Yes, I went there once – it's years ago now but it was great."

"The thing is, though, I wonder if we should leave it until Saturday. I've got to move the rest of my stuff tomorrow and settle into the other house. Would you mind, if we did it on Saturday? Hey, it can be a date."

Her face blazed crimson, she felt it, he saw it. They were both thrown into a fluster by her reaction. Mary pushed away from the table, taking refuge by bending to load the dishwasher, she mumbled at him.

"Well, if you'd rather do that. I just thought with it being your last night and all. Maybe it wasn't such a good idea." She felt the weight of him behind her; before he touched her arm, she knew he had come across from the table. She stood up but didn't turn, he was too close, there wasn't the space and she knew that if she was to spin round now there would be contact.

"I'm sorry Mary, that was a silly thing to say. I've embarrassed you, I'm sorry."

"Look, why don't I just cook us something to eat here, you buy a bottle of wine and we can have a relaxed, last evening?"

She tried to turn in the confined space pressing back against the dishwasher, the work top digging into her waist. Her head was lowered, his breath rustling her hair.

As if he only now became aware of the closeness, he stepped back sharply, swivelling away from her to collect the remaining breakfast debris. The air between them was buzzing, the atmosphere crackled with tension, and it was hard to breathe. She gulped and tried to get things back on an even keel.

"So, shall we do that then, it would be best probably. Then you can sleep here tomorrow night, if you like and move into your new place on Saturday morning. It'll be more relaxing for you."

"Great, yeah great. Shit, look at the time I'd better go."

The door slammed and she stood with her back against the cupboard unit, hands braced behind her. She felt dizzy, bewildered. He had hugged her on a couple of occasions and brushed past in the hallway, on the landing, but there was something else, today, something strange and electric and frightening.

She took a couple of steps to the table and lowered herself onto one of the wooden seats. It was because she was strung out wasn't it? She didn't want him to go. Didn't want to be on her own again and it had been a massive effort to keep it from him, as she knew she must, and really it would be better when it was over. She needed it to be over for it was tearing her apart inside and there was nothing to be done about it all.

Chapter 16

Friday passed slowly but too quickly. She wanted it to be tomorrow so that she could deal with it instead of living in a state of dread, but she also couldn't bear the thought of what it would mean. It was difficult to envisage how life would be afterward, on Sunday and Monday and all the days beyond. How long would it take to settle again, to regain her composure and her quiet acceptance of "alone," she didn't know.

Her eyes filled with tears at the thought of him leaving. Her colleagues were concerned, and she had to pretend that she had an eye infection.

She felt like a wrung-out rag climbing into the car in the late afternoon. Her heart was leaden and her spirit flat. It would have been easier to be going home to climb under the duvet in a darkened room and hide away. It wasn't possible, there was a carrier bag in the boot with the makings of a celebration meal, fancy hors d'oeuvres, some fillet steak, an expensive dessert thing to make them smile and feel good, things that would taste like sawdust and oil.

She pushed her key into the lock and leaned against the door. It swung inwards into the hallway and she gasped in surprise. Tied to the rail at the bottom of the stairs was a great bunch of balloons, each a different colour, waving and drifting on the ends of silky ribbons, "Thank You", over and over twisting in front of her eyes. The perfume reached her before she stepped inside but as she ducked under the coloured cords and reached the living room door, she spotted the vase of roses and lilies and greenery standing on the coffee table. There was a card beside them. She reached down and blinked away the tears that had blurred her vision. It was a Thank You card of course, a rabbit with a bunch of daisies grinning at her from the front page and inside under the scrolling text he had written with a green felt tip.

You are one of the most special people I have met
You have enriched my life with your kindness
Thank you
Jacob.

She gulped back a sob and raised a hand to her face to wipe away the moisture, and her lips quivered.

"Hey, you were supposed to like it."

She spun around and there he was behind her carrying two flutes of sparkling wine.

"Oh Jacob, you shouldn't have. You can't afford to do this. You really shouldn't have."

"Hey, I was going to take you out and then you…" He stopped. "Well, I would have spent more on a meal and I really wanted to see you smile. You've been a little glum the last few days, I thought –" He shrugged.

"Oh, Jacob it's lovely, truly. Thank you." She reached a shaking hand across the space between them and he gave her the glass of bubbly.

"Here's to your new home, Jacob."

"No, here's to you Mary. Thank you." They clinked the glasses and drank, and she summoned a tremulous smile as she wiped at the tears.

"I bought starters. They'll be great with this wine. I'll just put them on the plate." He took the bag from her hand and they plodded through to the kitchen.

Later, she would blame the wine, sparkling and fizzing in her blood, toying with her senses, she would blame the strangeness of her mood, the release of long held tension. Later, much later she would replay the scene over and over and look for reasons, excuses but she would come to see that it had been inevitable, for so long what happened now had been written and was unavoidable.

Chapter 17

Mary unpacked the plastic bag and put the steak in the fridge, the tiny starters looked pretty on the plate but as she transferred the last one it slipped and smeared across her fingers.

"Ooops."

She picked up the ruined treat and held it for Jacob to taste. As she tried to pop it into his mouth it slipped again. She snatched at it and he wrapped his fingers around her wrist. He leaned in and sucked the creamy mess from her finger ends. She gasped. He raised his eyes to hers and for a breathless moment time held.

He swallowed audibly but still held Mary's wrist. Their eyes locked. Heat and excitement built from deep in her gut. It was as if this moment had been but a breath away since she had looked up from the pavement the day of her fall. She didn't speak as his left arm circled her waist and pulled her closer. He sucked at the end of her finger, and the next and the next and the next.

She tipped her head and for just a moment closed her eyes. The feel of his tongue warm on her skin quickened her breathing. When she next looked, he had bent even closer. His breath stroked her face and as his mouth found hers, soft and warm, a pebble of worry and fear and longing somewhere deep inside melted and she leaned against him. He wrapped his other arm around her now and pulled her closer and yet closer and she felt as though she had come home.

The kiss was gentle but then she opened her lips slightly and he flicked his tongue into the edges of her mouth, a question which she answered readily. She had never kissed anyone but her husband like this and that had been such a long time ago that it was new again and thrilling.

He drew away and whispered, "Mary?" She couldn't speak and so just nodded, a tiny twitch of her head loaded with meaning and permission and promise.

He led her to the stairs but as they ducked under the strings of joyful balloons he stopped again, heat and sexual energy flooding from his body and he looked to her, deep into her eyes and he spoke again.

"Mary, is it okay?"

She smiled and they went upstairs and into his bedroom. It was good and a relief that he hadn't taken her into her own room, though she knew she would have gone, but this was better, this was right.

She sat on the edge of the mattress and he knelt on the floor in front of her. Leaning down to him she kissed his full lips again and then he reached to the front of her blouse and began to unfasten the buttons. With her arm loosely around his shoulders she drank in the nearness of him and the smell of him and the youth and strength. He shuffled forward on his knees and pushed the blouse down from her shoulders then pulled at the straps on her bra and she shrugged them off. He reached around and flicked at the fastenings.

As her breasts were freed from the lace and silk, she had a moment of panic and drew back covering herself with her hands. He leaned away from her holding up his palms giving her space, allowing her time. She looked at him kneeling before her, his hair dishevelled, his T shirt creased and marked with a splash of cream cheese and she felt her heart would burst with emotion.

She bent and slipped the leather of his belt through the buckle and then twisted the button through the hole and pushed down the zip on his jeans. He took her hands in his and half dragged, half pushed her backwards onto the bed and she shuffled on her behind across the covers and then swung her legs around and up. He stepped out of his pants and dragged the T shirt over his head. She had wriggled out of her trousers and in a moment of modesty grabbed at the corner of the duvet and pulled it over her. He slid underneath the covers, the firmness of his chest against hers, the bulge and swell of his muscles on top of her legs and stomach, and she closed her eyes and her mind to everything but the sensations.

At first she was hesitant, she stroked at his chest, almost hairless and sheened with youth. The end of day roughness on his chin was a counterpoint to the smoothness of lips against her mouth, her throat and the skin of her breasts. As he kissed her nipples, she raised her head to look down on the dark brown cap of his hair and he pulled back and grinned at her. His hands stroked at the rise of her belly and down to the promise of her thighs as she let her head fall back against the pillow. He raised himself above her and waited for the final permission, she shifted under him and the moan that escaped her throat was pure pleasure and guiltless joy lost in the moment and conscious only of his strength and the drive of his passion.

Chapter 18

Mary opened her eyes. She was full of stars, relaxed and peaceful. Her gaze wandered across the guest room as reality drove aside the bliss. Now it was hard to breathe, she turned her head. Surely this was a dream, the truth must be other than she knew it to be.

No.

He was there, asleep, his hair dishevelled on the pillow, an arm thrown carelessly across the covers, at ease and peaceful.

What had she done? What the hell had she done?

Sudden tears ran from her eyes and trickled across her face. She had to get away from this rumpled space, and even as she slid her feet to the floor other feelings crowded in, memories that were warm and mortifying at the same time. Shock made her shiver and still the ghost of what had happened whispered, his arms, his lips, his loving – generous and energetic, unquestioning and straightforward; Jacob making love to her.

Clothes were heaped on the carpet and she gathered them up scuttling past as quietly as possible. Once in the sanctuary of her own room and dragging on a bath robe, she struggled to calm her jittering mind and examine what had happened.

The wine had made her silly. The tension, the misery of his leaving had made her needy and vulnerable but it wasn't fair, wasn't true to imply that he had taken any sort of advantage. It had been mutual, all of it. He had given her every opportunity to step back, to regain the miserable sanity which would have been the right way to go. There had been no coercion; she had wanted it to happen.

Perched on the end of the bed she tried to calm herself and make sense of it all. What had he thought, this young man, how had he seen her? Had he wanted it to happen as much as she had? Events would say yes but then he was a young male, hormones raging, sex as much a need as food and drink. What would he think now, when he woke and remembered? Would he recall sagging arms, cellulite on her thighs, the appendix scar that puckered her belly? Would he think her ridiculous and laugh at her? A sob broke from her throat. How could she face him now?

He was moving, the quiet bang as the headboard shifted against the wall and then the creak of the one dodgy floorboard. The toilet in the tiny en-suite bathroom flushed, she heard the tap. The door whispered against the carpet.

She stood. There was no way to avoid this, to not see him, but if the earth had opened right then and offered a hole to lose herself in, she would have leapt without a moment's hesitation.

She heard him on the stairs.

"Mary, hey Mary, where are you?"

Her throat was too dry to answer. He was still calling, "Mary". Now the sound of feet running back up the staircase. She glanced down, pulled the robe tighter across her chest, ran fingers through sleep flattened hair and took one pace across the bedroom floor. He knocked and waited.

"Hey Mary, you in there?"

"Yes, I'm here, Jacob."

He pushed open the door. He wore his soft gym pants, his chest was bare, hair rumpled. He was grinning at her, a great goofy, little boy grin that lit his eyes, his face beamed with happiness. He stepped to her and wrapped her in his arms.

"Hi gorgeous. I wondered where you'd gone. I'm starving, what about that steak? Can we have that steak now?"

He bent and kissed her on the forehead, squeezing her in his embrace. She raised her eyes and saw nothing there of mockery or shame or embarrassment. All there was in the sparkling gaze was open good humour and yes, affection and friendship, and as the fear and worry melted away she was happy, so very, very happy.

Chapter 19

Mary washed salad, baked potatoes and then griddled the steak. She had sent Jacob into the little-used dining room with candles, condiments and instructions. Now they sat in the dim light, hours later than they had planned. Flickering shadows danced across the walls and quiet jazz stroked the edges of hearing. It was blissful and romantic and, for Mary, the nearest thing to perfection that she could imagine.

They raised their glasses of red wine and Jacob leaned across the corner of the table.

"To you, lovely, lovely lady. I am so very happy that I met you. I am so thankful that you let me into your home and I am so grateful that you have allowed me into your life."

As he spoke, his voice low, intimate and his eyes bejewelled by the candle flames, Mary felt the tears well against her eyelids.

He reached across and curled his fingers around her hand where it lay against the dark wood.

"Mary, I bet you are in turmoil. I am, and so you must be. I know that this must seem odd to you and a bit – well, a bit scary I suppose."

She didn't try to speak because she knew that her voice had flown and so she nodded dumbly. The tears escaped and with an embarrassed giggle she brushed them aside.

"Don't worry lovely, Mary, please don't worry. Tonight we will just leave things, let them sit as they are. You are very special to me and please believe me that I won't ever ask you to do anything that you don't want to. So, let's just enjoy this" – he raised his hand and waved it over the table settings – "let's just enjoy this, and then – when you are ready – we can talk about *us*. But for now relax and be happy. Yes?"

She was overwhelmed, how could such happiness, such kindness be hers. How was it that this young man had such maturity and sense whereas all she felt was surprise and confusion? It was wonderful and though there were doubts, fears and worries pushing at the gates of her mind she slammed them shut, looked into his eyes and smiled.

"I've got dessert, I don't know what it'll be like, a meringue thing."

"Yum, I love meringue, is it one of those with fruit?"

She nodded.

"Is there cream, oh please tell me you got cream?"

Another nod.

"Oh wow, how much better can this all get? I'm in heaven."

Though she knew that he was joking, and it was simply a turn of phrase, Mary felt it echo deep inside and for her, right now at this hour, on this night, she was in heaven.

They took their coffee into the lounge and lit more candles. Jacob threw himself onto the couch and reached out to take her hand and pull her down beside him. He wrapped both his arms around her and they lolled, sated, slightly fuzzy from the wine and the warmth and the aftermath of sex and they were at peace.

Mary wasn't stupid, she knew real life was still out there. There would be problems, a reckoning. What they had done wouldn't hurt anyone but she wasn't a teen, she had never taken sex, lovemaking, call it what you will, lightly. Until Jacob, she had only had sex with two other men. There had been her husband of course and a long-term boyfriend when they were students. She didn't know about Jacob, about young people these days. It wasn't to be doubted that they were more informed, more knowledgeable than she and her contemporaries had been, but how important it was to them, what it meant was something that she had never examined and now it seemed she would have to.

The tension, the sex and the food had made them sleepy, and struggle as they might they both felt their eyelids drooping. Jacob's head lolled forward, and he jerked upwards with a start. Mary stood and pulled him to his feet.

"Come on, I think we should leave the dishes and…" The sentence had no end. What should she say? "…erm."

"What do you want to do, Mary. We can go into my room if you like but if you want to, you know, sleep on your own it's fine as well."

She thought of her bed, cold and empty. Then she thought of his arms, the comfort of body heat in the night, the gentle sigh of his breath. A desperate loneliness overwhelmed her.

"Would it be okay if I came into your room? Just for now, tonight, I would like that. It's your last night and…"

"Come on, what about the dishes?"

"No, leave them, I can do them tomorrow."

He took her hand and they went together up the stairs and into the rather denuded room and as he curled his body around hers, his arms across her waist, they drifted away each into their own reality and each to their own thoughts and emotions.

Chapter 20

Coffee, rich and warm, the smell of it dragged Mary from the depths of sleep. Before she opened her eyes, she took stock. She could hear the shower running and smell the coffee, and the bed was warm beside her. She hesitated to fully emerge from the cocoon that wrapped her around. In her mind she replayed the earth shattering events of yesterday and thought quite simply - *Now what?*

Jacob was singing in the bathroom. As he turned off the water she heard a vaguely recognisable tune, something new that she had been aware of but hadn't really registered. As he filled in forgotten words with strange "dummy dumm de dumm" sounds she began to giggle and he opened the bathroom door to peer out at her.

"I'm sorry. Was there something funny?"

By this time she had pushed herself upwards to recline on the pillows. At the appearance of his shower reddened face, dark hair dripping onto the carpet and his skin glowing with heat all she could do was to laugh even louder and shake her head. He shrugged one shoulder and pursing his lips in a mock petulant gesture he turned, the movement caused him to drop an end of the towel and she had a glimpse of his behind as he stepped back behind the door. His legs were strong, muscular and covered with fine brown hair, his backside plump and rounded, a faint tan line above the waist and at the top of his thighs. He was beautiful, like a painting or a statue of a perfect young animal.

He had left a tray on the side table with a cafetiere and two mugs and a couple of the special chocolates that they hadn't eaten after the meal last night. She reached over and plucked up a liquid cherry. As the dark chocolate melted onto her tongue to be followed by the taste of bitter cherry and liqueur she snuggled back onto the pillows and pulled the duvet up to her chin. What a luxury, simply having someone else make her coffee in the morning and bring chocolate, liquid cherries at that, it was perfect.

Jacob ran from the bathroom door and leapt onto the bed. He had pulled on a pair of boxers but his skin was still damp and his hair dripped onto the pillowcase. He took her face in both hands.

"Morning, lovely lady." He kissed her lips, deeply and slowly. "Hmm, cherries, nice."

They sat side by side cradling mugs of coffee, Jacob slid his bare legs under the covers. With the heat of him beside her there came deep inside a delicious stirring such as she hadn't felt since the early days of marriage when it was all new and exciting and magical. The thought drew a mew of pleasure but also her eyes filled with sudden tears. How sad that this had been lost for so many years. She turned to the young man at her side, overwhelmed with emotion and unable to speak.

Without a word he put down his mug and turned and took her into his arms. "Don't cry lovely lady, please don't cry. It's all okay, there's nothing to worry about."

He cradled her gently until she was able to collect herself and turning her face up to smile into his eyes.

"Jacob, thank you." It was all she could think of to say. Her heart was so full. There were so many things that she wanted to tell him, so much to discuss and so many, so very many fears that must be verbalised and all she could say right then was, "Thank you".

He tipped his head to the side, his lips curved upwards in a small smile.

"No, thank you, ma'am."

It was all to be faced. It would be discussed and the fears must be recognised and dealt with but for just another few minutes Mary decided to gift herself the pleasure of sharing the morning with him. She tasted the bitter chocolate and rich creamy coffee and leaned against his firm body and listened to the bird song and early morning sounds from outside, in a world changed irrevocably since the last time she had walked in it.

Eventually, the coffee gone, the day already in full swing, she rolled onto her side and began to slide across the bed.

"Hey, where are you going?"

"Well, I thought, you know, it's nearly half past eight, time to get up."

"Why?"

"Well, there are things to do, stuff to sort out…" She shook her head, puzzlement drawing twin lines on her forehead.

"Well, if you like but erm…" He lifted the covers and she saw that he definitely had something on his mind that was far from tidying the dining room and sorting the laundry. For a moment she hesitated, long years of sense and order arguing with this urgent invitation to debauchery.

A time of youth, a backward glimpse of lazy mornings and careless weekends flicked across her memory. She looked at him for a few moments longer until, with a grin that was part mischievous little boy, part passionate man, he pulled her back under the cover. She lay in the middle of the bed as he rolled to her and stroked her goose-pimpled skin. He nibbled at the lobe of an ear. His hands caressed her breasts. The worry and fear and all the rest of

it slid away and was replaced by the utter joy of
lovemaking in the daylight, in a safe warm place, with a
person to whom she was learning to give her trust and,
maybe, her love.

Chapter 21

The lump in her throat was choking her. Mary tried to eat a piece of toast but it simply wasn't possible. She pushed her plate away.

"Aren't you eating your breakfast?"

Jacob had scoffed a bacon sandwich and was now making short work of toast spread thickly with butter.

"No, I'm not hungry."

As she watched him her stomach clenched. There were things that needed to be said, stuff that should be addressed but it was impossible to know where to start. Was he still leaving today, this morning, as was planned, and if so what did that mean?

"So, today?" She let the question hang in the air, vague and unfinished. He nodded.

"Yeah, well. Most of my stuff is already moved, there are just those two boxes in the hall. Steve said he might be able to come over later in his car and give me a lift with them but if not, I can get a taxi."

"Oh, right. I could always give you a lift."

It was the accepted thing to say wasn't it, the right thing to do? But really, she wasn't sure she could. How would it be to meet the others in his house, the young men

– oh and women – were there women? She didn't know. How would it be to say hello and cart his stuff in and leave him there. Would he introduce her as his friend, or maybe not at all? Tears filled her eyes, she was out of her depth, floundering in a sea of confusion.

She had hoped that he would stay now, after what had happened, but found it impossible to ask and if he did how were they to go on? What would she tell her friends, her family? She looked at him, his head bent over the plate. What was he feeling?

The chair tipped as she pushed away from the table, he started and half rose to his feet.

"Hey, are you okay?"

"Yes, yes, of course I'm fine."

Without a backward glance she left the kitchen, pounded up the stairs and locked herself in the bathroom where she lowered herself to the little wooden stool, wrapped her arms around her shivering body and let the tears come. He was leaving, okay it wasn't far away but it might as well be another country. She couldn't see him, not in his new place. It wasn't her territory and what did it say to her, the fact that he was carrying on with the plan, that he had made no move to discuss what had happened?

She dragged a piece of tissue from the toilet roll and dabbed at her streaming eyes.

Last night he had been wonderful. This morning in the sunlit bedroom there had been warmth but now it was as if none of it had happened. Yes, he had smiled at her when he came into the kitchen and thrown an arm about her waist, hugging her to him and planting a kiss on her cheek but nothing had been said, no discussion about the future, about the sex. He had been hungry, had gulped back a glass of water and then pushed bread into the toaster. Normal, ordinary. She hadn't known what to expect but this seemed wrong, or was it?

A great weight had settled in her stomach. Suddenly she retched and dropped to her knees on the tiles as she threw up the tea that she had drunk. She felt lost but it was time to regain control. She must face him, and trust him. She unfolded from her crouch on the floor, steeled herself and splashed cold water onto her face.

Jacob was clearing the dishes, stacking saucers and plates in the machine. As he heard her come back into the kitchen he straightened and turned.

"What do you want to do later? It'll only take me an hour or so to shift my gear and then we could go out if you like, go for lunch or a drink. Do you think?"

Butterflies fluttered in her belly, now hope soared.

"Oh, I hadn't thought. Are you sure, I mean you're busy, with the move and so on?"

"Yes, but as I said it won't take long and I'd like to spend some time with you, today."

"Tell you what, why not give me a call later, let me know how you are getting on and then we can see what's best."

"Great." He slammed the dishwasher door and as he strode out of the kitchen, hugged her again, a quick squeeze as he passed.

She heard him on the phone speaking to his friend, arranging collection of the boxes and then the click of his bedroom door and the boiler fired as he ran hot water in the bathroom.

He wanted to see her later, to spend time with her. She grinned as her spirits rose again.

She sat at the table and pulled her cooling drink towards her. Did she really need this chaos in her life, her world literally upended, her mind befuddled and emotions in turmoil? Then she remembered the feel of his arms around her, the brush of his lips warm against her skin and the heat of his body beside her in the bed and the answer had to be yes. Where was it leading? She didn't know; could she stop it? No, not now, she had tasted bliss and she wanted more, much more.

Chapter 22

The house was silent.

Jacob had left just minutes earlier, in the car with his friend. Laughing and waving, making a gesture with his hand, thumb and little finger extended, *I'll phone you*. She had turned from the drive, made her way back inside and closed the door, locking herself into the emptiness.

After her husband had died, when the undertaker had been and quietly taken him outside, sliding the wheeled trolley into the back of the black van, people had been there. There was the doctor, her sister, the neighbours. It had been overwhelming and Mary had slunk upstairs into the newly cleared room to sit quietly on the clean bed cover and feel Bill all around her. The sick smell was still there and the pills on the bedside table spoke of his struggle but beside that there was a memory of him when he was whole and strong. She had grasped at it in her grief and it had helped. Now there was no family, no embarrassed awkward neighbour, just a void and the spaces where Jacob had been.

She climbed the stairs and pushed through the door into the guest room which had been returned to its former status, waiting for a visitor who would probably never come. The bathroom was still warm and humid from his last use of it and the towels were damp. She lifted one to her face and inhaled the scent of him. He wasn't dead, he had gone for a while and she would see him later. He was going to call and they would meet, but right now the absence of Jacob was an assault to her senses. Two weeks he had lived with her, two days he had been her lover and she felt hollow and raw and forlorn, an old word but so perfect for the sense of total abandonment that she now felt. There were tears on her cheeks before she was aware that she had shed them, and the sob that gasped its way from her throat was a shock.

She must keep control. She must trust him to call as he had promised.

In a flurry of activity, she gathered up the towels and sheets, the mark of his presence, and thrust them into the washing machine. She thumped back upstairs with the vacuum cleaner and a box of polish and dusting cloths. Next was an assault on the windows, spraying the artificially scented fluid onto the glass. She ran through to her own room and turned on the radio, loud, and then back to scour the bathroom, spray polish on the furniture and clean the carpets. She would make the house as it was, she would reclaim her spaces.

How she came, sometime later, to be sitting on the floor in the corner of the guest room she couldn't say but there she was. He was going to call, he said so. She ran through to the other room and picked up the handset, the dial tone mocked her. He would call, he had only been gone an hour, maybe two.

But what then, when they had met, had a meal and a few drinks, what then? Would he leave her in town, bring her home, would he expect her to go back to his shared rooms? This was madness, she wasn't a young girl, a student. She couldn't go out on a date with Jacob and then leave him with a kiss in a darkened doorway, a promise to call in the week. Women of her age didn't behave like this, they just didn't.

The phone rang and she scuttered to her room banging her leg on the corner of the bed in her haste.

"Hello." Her heart was pounding.

"Hi there, it's me."

"Jane?"

"Yeah, hey sorry who were you expecting?"

"Oh, sorry no. I just didn't think it would be you. Sorry, I banged my leg. Hi, how are you?"

"I'm good, yeah fine. I wondered if you were busy."

"Busy?"

"Yes, I wondered if you could do me a favour."

"Oh, erm. Well yes of course. If I can."

"My blasted car has to go into the garage and Alan has gone to his mother's. Could you give me a lift back do you think?"

"Oh, I don't – well, I mean, what time?"

"Now really, look it's okay if you're busy. I know it's short notice and all, but you're not usually busy at the weekend and I thought maybe we could pop into town after and have a bite – my treat, and then you could take me back. They said it was only a little job, just a couple of hours. Don't ask me about it 'cos I have no idea."

"Thing is though, I was going to erm, do some stuff, well maybe, I wasn't sure." She couldn't think what to say. Why was that? Why not just tell Jane that she was meeting someone? Her stomach flipped, and her throat had dried. "Yes, of course I will, of course. Come on over and then I'll follow you to the place. Yes, that's fine."

"Are you sure?"

"Of course, yes, it's fine."

"Brilliant. See you in about twenty minutes then. You're a pal."

Mary replaced the handset and sat staring at the grey plastic; her mind was empty and her senses were numb.

Now what was she going to do?

Chapter 23

"Right, where do you want to go for lunch?" Jane slid into the passenger seat and clicked on her seat belt. "They said that I can pick the car up about four o'clock. That's okay isn't it?"

Mary's heart sank. The whole afternoon taken up with this favour and no chance to contact Jacob. She had hoped that he might ring as she sat and waited in the car park of the garage but no matter how hard she had stared at her mobile it had remained resolutely silent. Now they were heading into town and lunch and the shops. She didn't want to shop, and she didn't believe it would be possible to eat or to sit and chat with Jane with her mind so much in another place. She forced a smile.

"Yes, 'course that's fine. Are we going to the town centre or would you prefer the mall? Have you got anything specific you want?"

"No, no I just thought a bit of window shopping, some lunch and a good old natter. I haven't seen you for ages."

"No, well okay. So how about the Bistro then?"

"Yeah, great. So, what have you been up to?"

As the car turned out of the parking place and into the road, Mary's mobile tweeted. Before she had a chance to react Jane had grabbed it from the little hollow in the dashboard.

"It's a text, shall I read it to you? It's from someone called Jacob."

"NO! Oh sorry, heh where did that come from, sorry."

"Oh well excuse me." Jane replaced the phone with a clatter. "I was only trying to help."

"Yes, yes, of course you were. I'm sorry I didn't mean to shout. It's this traffic; it's reminded me why I get the bus into town."

Her friend didn't answer. An atmosphere of pique and offense settled in the little car.

"Really, I'm sorry Jane, I didn't mean to shout. Anyway, yes could you have a look for me, see what it says."

It wasn't what she wanted. Not in a million years did she want Jane reading her text from Jacob but couldn't bear the atmosphere and so compromised and mentally crossed her fingers that it would be bland, non-specific.

"Well, if you're sure."

Her friend's inquisitiveness overrode the slight and in moments the phone was back in her hand bipping and squeaking as she opened the text folder.

"Hello lovely lady. Sorry 2 b late. Can we meet l8ter? xx"

For the first time in her life Mary fully understood the term "a pregnant pause". Neither of them spoke. Jane slid the phone back into its home on the dash.

"Right, so. Jacob?" She waited. Mary could feel the heat spreading from her neck and into her cheeks.

"Yes. He's a friend. Actually, I hadn't realised how long it is since I'd seen you. This all happened since the last time."

It wasn't strictly true but she was thinking on her feet, trying to find her way out of the sudden maze.

"He - stayed with me, just for a couple of weeks. Moved out today as a matter of fact, this morning, just

before you rang. He wanted to take me out for a meal –
just a thank you sort of thing.”

“Lovely lady?” Jane had crossed her arms and turned
her head to stare at the side of Mary’s blushing face.
“Lovely lady?” she repeated.

“Heh. Yes, idiot, he started calling me that. He was
stuck, you see, for a bed. He had to get out of the place he
was in and his new place wasn’t available ‘til today and so I
put him up. He was grateful, you see, so that’s why –
Lovely lady. A bit daft but, well you know, nice in a way as
well.”

“So, who is he then? Somebody from work?”

“No, not from work. He’s just a friend.”

“What, a friend of Bill’s?”

“No, you know, just a friend, somebody I met.”

“Well, where did you meet him, you never go
anywhere?”

“Oh, thanks for that.”

“No, no you know what I mean, you don’t go many
places where you would meet men do you? Sorry that
came out wrong.”

“Tell you what, let’s get to the Bistro and then I’ll tell
you all about it yeah?”

“Oh, don’t feel you have to, I don’t want to be nosey.”

Of course she did, it was obvious there was going to be
no way to avoid this conversation. Mary had bought a little
time, a space to get her thoughts straight but she was
overwhelmed by the need to respond to the text.

As soon as they had been seated in the restaurant Mary
made a dash for the ladies. Inside the cubicle she opened
the message. She typed quickly – *Sorry. Was driving. Would
love to meet you but I am in town with Jane. Sudden plan. Can I
call you later on?* – Send.

She waited for a while but when it became clear that he
wasn’t going to respond at once, she had to make her way
back to Jane who was reading the menu and ordering
sparkling water, bread and dips.

"Do you want a drink? I wasn't sure with us both driving later."

"No, no absolutely. Water will be fine. Have you decided what you're eating?"

"Hmm – pasta. I thought I'd have a proper lunch. Alan won't be back tonight so I didn't want to cook."

"Right. Well I think I might just have a salad."

"Oh yes, you've got a date." The comment was followed by a sharp laugh.

"Well no, but if I do meet him, I suppose we might eat, so –"

The phone pipped at them. Mary dragged it from her pocket.

Ok. Call me. Am free now. Go out or takeaway.
Up to you. Xxx

"Don't mind me. Answer it if you want to."

Jane had returned to her study of the menu looking annoyed. Mary would normally refuse to text or talk on the phone at table but she couldn't help herself.

Takeaway great. Home by about six at the latest.
Come round after that. X

Before there was any chance of a reply, she made a show of pushing the phone into the bottom of her bag.

"So, come on then. You said you'd tell me all about it. Who is this mystery man?"

"Well he's just someone who was stuck for a room as I said. I put him up in my spare and now he's gone and just wanted to take me out to say thank you. That's about it really."

"So, how come you're beetroot red and you've shredded that napkin?" She glanced down and was horrified to see the tissue in pieces on the table.

"Oh crumbs, I didn't know I was doing that."

Jane reached across the cloth and laid a hand over Mary's.

"Hey, it's okay you know. If you've met someone, I'm glad for you. You don't have to hide it from me. You're still young you should meet more people." With a final squeeze of her fingers she then let go and reached for the chilled water.

"That's so nice Jane. Thank you."

"So, what's he like then?"

"He's really sweet."

"And where did you meet him?"

"Oh, well it's a bit embarrassing to be honest. I fell over and he helped me, and then he came into work, purely by chance, and well that was how I found out about his flat and so on. Well actually no that's not right but anyway I met him again on the bus and that was when he told me about his room and so I said that I had a spare."

"So how long ago was this then?"

"As I said round about the last time I saw you."

"And you didn't know him before that?"

"No."

"Oh well, don't you think that was a bit, well, a bit irresponsible?"

"Irresponsible. Oh, I suppose it was in a way but he is so lovely and I just never had any worry about it. I do understand what you mean but it wasn't like it seems. Well, he's not, oh I don't know the word, threatening. He's not threatening. He's so nice."

"But if you didn't know anything about him, it was a bit soon."

"Yes, yes I know but he's so young." It was out before she realised what she was about to say, so very keen to paint him in a good light she had let slip the one thing that was worrying her.

"Young?"

"Yes, he's only young. He's twenty. Well, twenty-one to be accurate."

"Oh, crikey. I'm so sorry Mary I bet you thought I was being mean. I didn't realise. The way you were and then that Lovely Lady thing – I thought you were having a bit of a thing. Oh, I'm sorry, I jumped to a conclusion."

"No, no it's fine." She was going to get away with it, wasn't she?

She would have done if the phone hadn't pinged right then and the glass hadn't been so close, and as she grabbed her bag and spilt the water and tried to rescue the whole thing with shaking hands, the ensuing chaos said more about her mental state then any outright confession would have done.

Chapter 24

When the spilled water had been cleared and the table tidied Mary looked at her friend and knew that now was the time to face the music and get the situation out into the open. She took a deep breath, steadied her nerve.

"Actually Jane, I am, I mean we are – we did, you know – what you said."

"How old did you say he was?"

"He's twenty-one." As she said it Mary raised her eyes and looked at Jane directly, she didn't blink and though her heart was pounding she kept her gaze steady and her hands curled in her lap.

"Twenty-one. He's twenty-one – Christ." Jane swallowed hard, her eyes were popping, her mouth gaped. "He's a kid, Mary he's a kid. Tell me you're making it up. Please tell me it's not true."

Mary held her peace as she watched Jane process the information.

"You have got to be kidding me. You let a boy, that's what he is, a boy, you let him come and live with you. A kid you didn't know and then, then – No. Are you really telling me that you had sex with him? Oh, I don't believe this. How could you? What were you thinking? Mary tell me it's not true."

"It is true. I met him; he came to stay with me. I was drawn to him, I couldn't help it and then when he, well when we – oh it wasn't like you're making it out to be. It was wonderful. He is wonderful."

"No, no stop there. I don't want to hear any more. I can't believe this. I'm sorry Mary, I really am but I don't think I can talk about this with you. I'm shocked. You're old enough to be his mother, his mother. Oh – yuk, it's as if I slept with one of Millie's friends. It's not right, it's – well yes, it's disgusting." Jane leaned down and picked up her bag.

"Where are you going?"

"I don't know, I can't stay here with you. You appal me." And then it came, the final thrust. "Just exactly what do you think Bill would have said, eh, your husband, how do you think he would have reacted? Well, I thought I knew you, but I was wrong. I would never have believed it, never in a million years. It's horrible."

With that she pushed back the chair and flounced from the little restaurant leaving Mary with tears rolling down her face, hands shaking and bile rising in her throat. As she bent to retrieve her things the phone pinged again.

See you later? xx

She ran out of the building and down towards the car park. Her mind was in turmoil. Jane had vocalised all the thoughts that she had been trying to quell, opened the Pandora's Box of fear and guilt. She reached the car park but her feet carried her on down the road, on and on, blindly away from the awful scene, on and on thrusting between Saturday shoppers and loitering teens anywhere that was away from what had just happened.

By now she was crying wildly, attracting interested glances from people as she hurtled past. She was gasping, her coat flying behind her, bag dangling madly from her arm. Still she ran on, past the shops, out away from the town centre and up to the park, in through the gates and down towards the lake. By now the headlong flight had eased. Shortness of breath slowed her and she plonked onto a wooden bench, lowered her head into her hands and sobbed as she hadn't done in all the years since first hearing that she was to lose her beloved husband.

Chapter 25

The storm passed. Gulping and wiping at the tears on her face, Mary tried to regain her senses. What had she expected, really?

It, the wonder of Jacob, had happened quickly. It had all been so quick, so unexpected that she hadn't thought beyond the moment, those precious moments in his arms, wallowing in the delight of sex and amazement.

Of course, there had to be a reckoning. Life had taught her that pleasure brought pain. There was always a time to pay and here it was.

She tried to clear her mind. After the horrible things that she had heard, how did she really feel? Was Jane right? Had what they had done been wrong, had it been disgusting? She wrapped her arms around herself, swallowed hard and blinked back the new tears.

The phone pinged.

It was Jacob.

> *Are you on schedule? I'm free now; let me know when*
> *you get home. Have a nice day with your friend.*

She didn't know how to reply. Tell him not to come? Turn him away and move beyond him, draw back from the new intimacy. She took a deep breath and glanced around. The park was deserted. The only sounds were the birds in the trees and shrubs, and the shush of the water against the hulls of the little rowing boats all tied together beside the jetty. It was peaceful and pleasant but she couldn't stay. She would see him tonight and talk to him. She needed time before then to sort her scrambled thoughts.

Jane had been her friend for a long time and had seen her through so much. She had been the strong arm to lean on, and seeing the shock and the disgust on her face had been painful. If that was the way everyone would react — her mum and dad, her other friends — then maybe it really was wrong. It had been a mistake, irresponsible. This was a warning. She had taken steps down a forbidden path and must turn back before it was too late. Dabbing at her face with a soggy tissue she trudged back to the car. Once inside fished in the bottom of the big handbag to find her phone.

On my way home. See you soon.

As she responded to his text there was a stone in place of her heart and a lump of sadness choked her throat. It was going to have to stop now, what had she been thinking? A boy, as Jane had said, just a boy and surely then, out of bounds. She had been tasting forbidden fruit. She would see him one more time and then let him go. She knew that a face to face conversation was the only way to do it, although the thought was torture.

There was no point trying to dash aside the tears. More followed more, they just had to be allowed to flow, so she sniffed and snivelled and raised a hand from the steering wheel to clear her vision when the weeping filled her eyes. She parked in her drive and staggered through the front door. Dropping her coat and bag she thudded upstairs to the bedroom and collapsed face down across the bed and indulged at last in an unfettered bout of crying.

Why was she crying? The thought inveigled its way into her roiling mind. For herself? But why? She rolled onto her back. She was crying because of the embarrassment. Okay, was that all? No, she was crying because of Jacob. Wishing right now that she had never met him, and been drawn to him and now must let him go. The tears were for all of it, the passion and the pain and the misery of realising that she had made a stupid mistake that may well have lost her an old and well-loved friend.

She heard the slam of the front door and shot up from the bed in panic.

"Hi, Mary, it's me. I used my key. I hope that's okay."

His footsteps pounded on the stairs as he ran up to where she was desperately trying to repair her ravaged face.

"Give me a minute, I'll be out in a sec."

"Oh, okay, can I put the kettle on?"

She heard him thump back to the kitchen and then the water running. She went through to the bathroom and stared at herself in the mirror. Her eyes were red and sore looking, still swimming with unshed tears. No matter, she must talk to him right away. She held a cold cloth to her eyes to sooth them and then turned to go and join him in the kitchen. She would tell him straight away, tackle the thing quickly, she would be strong.

Chapter 26

Jacob looked up from where he was pouring the tea. He smiled and it tore at her heart. He put down the pot.

"Hey, what's matter, what happened?"

As his arms went around her, she stiffened. He pulled back still holding onto her, bending to look into her eyes. For long moments emotion stole her voice, then she gulped and stepped away. If she allowed herself to melt against him, to listen to the thud of his heart and relax into the heat of his body then she would be lost.

She must be strong.

"Jacob, I'm sorry." She yearned for the feel his skin against her hands. She stepped further away. "I'm sorry, you mustn't come here. I don't think you should visit me. I think that…"

She couldn't continue. He embraced her and she leaned in and took the comfort.

"I'm sorry Jacob, we've made a big mistake. I've made an error of judgement. We need to stop it. We can't do this."

"We can't do what?"

"See each other, be together. We can't have a relationship, we mustn't."

"Why?"

It was a simple question, innocent. But he hadn't been there to see the look on Jane's face. While Mary had been suffering an agony of embarrassment and grief he had been moving into his new home, spending time with his friends. Coming to the situation cold he had reacted with honesty and now she had to explain, somehow.

"Well it's wrong."

"What's wrong? I don't know what you mean. What are you talking about?" He led her to the table, pulled a chair away for her to sit and then knelt in front of her on the floor. He held her hands in his and looked into her eyes. He searched her face for answers and she searched her mind for ones to give that would be kind.

"I saw Jane, my friend," she said. "I told her about us."

He tilted his head to one side and narrowed his eyes.

"I don't know how it happened, it just slipped out. I told her that I had met you and that you stayed here."

He nodded but he had let go her hands now.

She was aware that on top of everything else she had actually been indiscreet. Discussing their relationship had been a betrayal in itself. Shame reddened her cheeks as she tried to continue.

"I don't know how it happened and I think now that I was wrong but, I told her, you see. I told her about us."

"Yeah?" He was waiting for more. She was going to have to be more specific.

"I told her that we slept together, Jacob. I told Jane about that. I'm sorry, I know I shouldn't have but I did."

"Yeah, I see. It isn't her business is it, so what's the problem?"

"Well, she was appalled, she was disgusted. She stormed out of the restaurant."

"Why?"

"What do you mean why?"

"Well, I mean why did she storm out of the restaurant for one thing but, why was she appalled and disgusted? Has she never had sex then?"

He laughed as he said it. This conversation wasn't going the way that Mary had expected, and she was floundering now. There was a gulf between them, he didn't understand. How could he not understand?

"Well, of course she has. It's not that, not the sex, well it is but not only that. It's us, don't you see? It's us – you and me having sex."

"Why?"

"Oh Jacob, don't be cruel, you know why, surely you know why. Please this is so hard for me, don't be mean."

He drew back his hands.

"I'm sorry Mary, I just don't understand. So you told Jane we had sex and she thought that was disgusting, but I don't see. Nothing we did was disgusting. We just had sex, actually I rather thought we made love but whatever. What was disgusting? Is she a Catholic, is it because we're not married? Shit, that's so old fashioned."

"No, well yes – I suppose that's part of it but don't you see it's us, you and me? The age difference."

"Oh for goodness sake, don't be silly. It can't be, well I mean, how can that make any difference? No, no you've got it wrong."

"No, I haven't. She said as much, said you are just a boy and that I'm old enough to be your mother and she's right, isn't she?"

"Well, I suppose so if you want to just count years, but – well, so what? What has it got to do with her anyway? I know she's your friend and all but, really, she needs to get real. I'm not a schoolboy, you didn't force me, nothing like that. Oh, come on now, don't start crying again. This is all silly, it's a nonsense. This is what happens though isn't it? When you let other people in, it spoils things.

"Unless of course you really mean it and you don't want to see me again. But make sure it's for your own reasons, Mary, and not because of what some busybody said to you in a restaurant."

She studied him for a moment; his beautiful face below hers where he knelt on the hard tiles, his look open and clear, his expression honest. There was something else there though, behind his eyes, impatience, possibly anger, and why not? He hadn't asked for this. She had been gossiping and he had a right to be upset. Didn't he?

"I'm sorry, Jacob."

She bent to him and kissed him. It was instinct and need, and as their lips met, the trouble and fear took wing and left her. All that was left was the feel of his breath on her face and the strength of his arms as he cuddled her close. She relaxed against him and knew that she wouldn't let him go. Not for Jane, not for appearance's sake, and not for Bill who she didn't believe would deny her happiness, even if it came from a strange and unlooked for place.

Chapter 27

He stayed, they sent out for pizza and then they made love. If Jacob noticed that his room had been cleaned and reinstated as the guest accommodation, he didn't mention it. He made no attempt to take Mary to her own bed, though after the trauma of the day and the new resolve it had led to, she had already decided that she didn't mind where they went as long as it was with him.

She pushed the painful memories away. Time enough to deal with it when he wasn't here and wasn't kissing her and smoothing away the worries with his caresses.

After the sex he fell asleep and Mary lay beside him in the tumbled bed, calm and relaxed. Today had shocked her to the very core of her being but now, in this warm space with Jacob, she didn't care what anyone thought. Surely this peace, this happiness, couldn't be wrong. She would grasp this unexpected measure of joy in her life even though it was late in coming.

Later they went back downstairs; wrapped in robes they drank wine and listened to music in the candle lit living room until it was late and the street outside was silent. He dragged himself from the settee and stood looking down at her.

"I'm going now, Lovely Lady. Shall I see you tomorrow? Don't worry about Jane she'll probably come around but, well you know, sometimes it's best to try to keep private things private – it's something you women seem to have trouble with – eh?"

She was going to retort to the chauvinistic remark but he was leaving and there had been enough friction for one day.

"Can you not stay tonight?"

"No, I need to get back. We've got an early start tomorrow. Steve's taking me to the gym and then we're meeting some of the others for a drink. You can come if you like, well maybe not to the gym," he grinned, "but for a drink. It'll just be the pub but you can meet some of my friends and it'll be fun."

She was already shaking her head.

"I can't. I don't think I can do that, Jacob. Do your friends know, about me, about us?"

"Well, I haven't made a thing about it you know, I don't gossip, not like some people!"

He smiled as he said it but she was aware now that he had referred to her conversation with Jane several times. Was he more put out than he was letting on? She studied his face and saw nothing there that could be construed as anger or disapproval but yet, there was something. He was collecting his things together and heading for the stairs.

"Steve knows I was living here. Well, I suppose the others do as well but I haven't been carving our initials on the door frame or anything like that."

He turned back and came to sit beside her. His face was serious, and he reached and took her hand.

"Mary, what do you want to do here? I mean, for me this is great, it is what it is. We like each other; we've got a connection, yes?"

She nodded.

"We like being together, we enjoy the sex, I don't know why you're worrying. As far as I'm concerned you are not some big secret. No, I haven't told all my mates that we've got a thing going on, but that's only because I don't talk about stuff like that. Why don't you come and meet them? If you like I can just tell them you're a friend but honestly you don't need to hide anything. We don't have to sneak around; this isn't a nasty little affair where other people are going be hurt. Come on, meet my mates, come to the pub," he said.

Her heart was pounding. He was so open and honest, so much better than she was. As far as Jacob was concerned, they were simply living and enjoying it. For him there was no hidden agenda, no subterfuge. They were loving friends engaged in a relationship, could it really be that the age difference mattered to him not at all? It all seemed too good to be true.

"I don't think I can, not yet."

As the words left her mouth, she remembered again the ugly look on Jane's face, and it brought her up short. Maybe hiding what was happening was just another version of Jane's prejudice? If Jacob had been in the world for just a few more years would she not now be planning what to wear to meet his friends? Could it be she was buying into the attitude she had been so hurt by? What other reason could she have for not going for a drink with a friend, except that she was ashamed to be seen with him or that it was wrong. She wouldn't do that – she owed him more.

"I'll tell you what, why don't you send me a text when you get to the pub, in case there's a change of plan? Send me a message and let me know where you are and I'll come and meet you." She pulled a wry face as she spoke, a gentle way to let him know this was costing her effort but he smiled back at her and leaned to give her a peck on the cheek.

"Great stuff, we'll be going local so don't bring the car and then maybe later we can go for something to eat."

"No, don't let's do that, let me cook for you. I'd like to."

"Great, sounds like a perfect plan. Right, if I go now I'll catch the last bus. See you tomorrow, yes?"

She nodded and stood to walk with him to the door.

She watched his indistinct silhouette through the mottled glass as it wavered and faded in the light from the streetlamp. Back in the living room she tidied up the glasses and turned off the music. She wrapped her arms around herself. *"Okay, you're committed now lady,"* she muttered quietly. *"Heaven knows where this is all going to end. What a day."* She reached and turned out the light.

Chapter 28

Mary had tossed and turned till the sheets were a tangle around her legs and the pillow felt as though it was stuffed with old egg boxes. As the rising sun glinted through the gaps in the curtains, she clomped downstairs to make coffee and toast. Breakfast eaten she went for a walk through the quiet Saturday morning streets but the sleeping neighbourhood did little to soothe her nerves and now back in the house she was treading up and down the short hallway.

This had to be done, there was no other choice, but drumming up the courage to lift the phone and dial Jane's number was proving impossible.

As soon as her head had hit the pillow in the darkness last night the scene in the restaurant had begun to play. A continual reel, each time with the dreadful bitter ending.

It had to be addressed; leaving things as they stood just wasn't an option. It was now half past eight and probably a reasonable time to phone. She reached out and lifted the handset.

"Hello?" At the sound of her friend's voice Mary's mouth dried and all the well-rehearsed words flew like dust in the wind. "Hello?" She must speak or Jane would assume it was a sales call and hang up the phone. It would be even more difficult to dial a second time. Mary cleared her throat.

"Jane, it's me. It's Mary." She heard nothing.

"Are you there Jane?"

Oh please don't let her hang up on me, please, please. She rolled her shoulders trying to ease the tense muscles. Her hand coiled around the banister rail for support. She needed to hold something solid, needed to feel grounded.

"Jane, I need to speak to you, I need us to talk. Please."

"I don't think that there is anything much to say Mary. I said all I needed to yesterday."

"Yes, yes, but I would like to explain. I need a chance to make you understand. Please Jane can we meet, or I could come to your house?" By now tears were trickling down her cheeks and her voice quavered.

"No, I don't want you to come here but I'll listen to what you have to say now. I don't think I want to meet you though."

"Oh, well okay. I just thought that maybe if I explained about him, about Jacob, maybe I could make you understand. You seemed so shocked yesterday and I think I see why, I think so but well, I talked to him last night and…"

"You talked to him? You talked to this kid about me? Well, I would prefer if you didn't, thank you."

"No, not about you, well not exclusively. He came over and I was so upset and of course he wanted to know why and so I had to tell him. He didn't see why you were so shocked and so I thought maybe if we talked about it you could come to feel differently." She was gabbling, she knew it. She took a breath and slowed her breathing. "I have always valued our friendship, Jane. I would hate for this to come between us."

"You're a fool, Mary, a fool."

"What?"

"You heard me, you're an idiot. Come on now, be honest with yourself. This boy is twenty years old and you actually think, you truly believe, that he loves you?"

"Well no, no love hasn't been mentioned, I mean it's not like that."

"So, what is it like then? What do you think he's getting out of it, really? All the young girls there are about these days, all the gorgeous teens and you think that he'd rather have sex with you, a middle-aged widow. Oh, come on, be realistic, he's after something, you mark my words. I bet in a week or two he'll be wanting to borrow some cash or to move back in, to borrow your car, to get a loan with you as guarantor. You mark my words Mary, he's after more than just a granny grope."

"Oh!" As she threw the handset back onto the cradle Mary collapsed in a shuddering heap onto the hall carpet. Rocking back and forth she sobbed.

"Oh, how could you, how could you?"

As the minutes passed fury replaced the anguish. There was no room for doubt now, no lingering hope; the friendship with Jane was surely over. No matter what happened she couldn't consider someone who could make such judgements, utter such hurtful and damning words, as her friend.

The anger brought her to her feet and she ran up the stairs, slammed into the bathroom and stood under the shower. *Well sod you, Jane, you and your small mind and your evil tongue.* She sank into the tub and as the hot water beat down on her head, she lowered her face and sobbed.

Chapter 29

The shower didn't calm her fury so she vented her spleen on eggs and butter, sugar and chocolate, turning out an Anger Gateaux. By the time the kitchen had been cleaned and the dishes put away she felt almost normal. Whenever the conversation with Jane wheedled its way into the forefront of her mind, and it did – often, she began to fume again. It was the unfairness of it that hurt so much. That Jane would make such terrible judgements about someone she had never met. Now she regretted throwing down the phone, but it was obvious that no matter how long they had spoken she wouldn't have been able to turn Jane's viewpoint around. It was so very venomous and fixed.

Life would be strange and sad without her old friend but it couldn't be helped. It was time to go and meet Jacob and his crowd and take life a bite at a time and get through this turmoil.

She went to the bedroom and in no time at all the bed and floor were littered with clothes. Slacks, skirts, blouses and jackets. All had been tried on and rejected and now Mary stood in front of the mirror in her underwear, panic in her eyes and best jeans in her hands. The very fact that she had "best" jeans was the thought that was now making her blush. None of the other people there today would have jeans kept for days when it was necessary to look smart but casual, expensive denim that fitted well and had fancy stitching on the back pockets. She was what she was, older, more careful about her appearance and there was no help for it – she had "best" jeans and that was what she would wear.

She pulled on a soft blue sweater and black boots and actually thought the result was okay. She hoped that her look avoided the dreaded "frump" but also steered clear of looking like a lump of mutton trying too hard. In her mind's eye she formed a picture of the groups of youngsters who had frequented the pub on Sundays when she had gone there, back in the days of Bill. They had all looked so very much the same, muted colours, lots of grey but they exuded something, a comfort in their own skin that she was longing to find now.

When the message pinged into her phone, she hoped that it was to say that the meet was cancelled, but it was a simple text:

The Oak, we are there now. See you soon. J x

She ran down the stairs, picked up her bag and phone and left the house quickly, before there was a chance to think about it. It was a ten-minute walk to the pub through bright sun warmed streets and by the time the red roof and whitewashed walls came into view a bilious energy was rumbling in her tummy and her heart fluttered with nerves. She pushed open the door and peered into the gloom. A large group of them sat at a big table in the square bay window. She spotted Jacob and raised a hand. He made his way across the room and took hold of her arm leading her towards the noisy group.

"This is Mary." A couple of the young men moved closer together so that she could slide in next to the seat Jacob had been using.

"Hi, Mary. I'm Steve, I live with Jake."

"Hi, I'm Gary." They didn't shake hands but smiled and nodded at her and then went back to their conversations.

"Hi I'm Judy." A pretty, long haired girl sandwiched between three others waved at her. "Sandy, Clare, Phil." And so it went on until they had all acknowledged her arrival. She smiled and nodded at them.

"What do you want to drink?" Jacob had pushed his hand into his pocket to draw out a handful of cash. Mary wasn't sure what the arrangement would be. Were they all buying their own drinks? Was there a kitty as had been the way when she was young? There was so much to find out and now she felt old and out of place.

"We all get our own. That way you don't have to worry, you can have just what you like. What would you like?"

She glanced at the table. An assortment of glasses littered the wet wood but mostly they were pints of lager.

"I'll have a half of lager please. Is that okay?"

"Yes of course, hey relax, you're supposed to be having fun." He stepped away to weave through the crowd at the bar. Her every nerve was on high alert. She was out of her depth.

"So, you're Mary?" She turned towards the voice.

"Yes, I'm erm."

"You're his landlady right, well you were. He told us about you, he said you were a great cook. Hey if you ever need another lodger can I move in?"

"Oh, erm I don't really."

"It's okay I'm joking. Well mostly."

Jacob's voice came from just behind her.

"Hey Steve back off, if anyone's moving back in it'll be me, right?"

He placed the glass in amongst the others and sat beside her on the bench giving her arm a reassuring squeeze. She smiled at him and picked up the drink gulping back a third of it. She tried to follow some of the conversations flowing back and forth but coming in late much of it was already out of reach.

The boy who had spoken earlier turned to her again. "So, Mary, what do you do?"

"I work at the doctor's, a receptionist." It sounded so very dull. Jacob leaned around her. "Steve's mum is a nurse, isn't she, Steve?"

"Yeah."

"His mum, oh right." He had meant nothing, probably hadn't even thought about it but with that one statement Jacob had pigeonholed her in the most cruel way.

"Hey Mary, don't you live near here?" One of the other girls called across the table, "you're local yes?"

"Well yes."

"Great so where's the best place to get Chinese?"

"Oh, the Hot Wok I think."

"No, no that's wrong. The Silver Palace is much better."

"Ah but at the Hot Wok you get free wantons."

"Yeah?"

"Yeah." She grinned back at the interested faces and with that tiny move in the conversation she found herself a part of the whole, just another one in the group and she began to unwind and relax. She turned and looked at Jacob; he was sprawling on the seat totally at ease. Where did such confidence come from, where could she find it? It was beyond her.

Chapter 30

Side by side they strolled the quiet suburban streets.

"So, did you have a good time?" Jacob turned his head and grinned at her.

"Yes, thank you it was lovely. Your friends are really nice." It was a lie of course but how could she say anything else? How could she say to him, *No Jacob I felt odd and out of place, I didn't understand a lot of what they were saying and except for a few minutes now and again I felt as though I were stranded in a land of aliens?*

Was it her? Well probably. She had believed herself fairly up to date with current thinking, she knew the new films that came out and, though she wouldn't wear much of it, was aware of current fashion trends but now realised that it was all superficial. The opinions, beliefs and preferences of his friends were simply from another place. She was sorry to have gone. Now, revealed in cruel starkness, were all the differences between her generation and his. Her heart was sad, and she felt very silly. Jane was right, she was a fool.

As they turned into the road where her house stood Jacob reached and took her hand, she let her own fingers lie softly in his. There was the other thing as well nibbling away at the edge of her mind, the collisions of two comments from two different places but heading in a dreadful way towards a nasty conclusion. Jane had shrieked at her that it was only a matter of time before he wanted something from her, something more than the friendship and the passion – money, a loan, to move back into the house. At that time, she had smacked the thought aside. Of course Jane didn't know him and anyway if he did ask to come back, she would welcome him, would welcome his presence in her private world. Why was it then that as he made the comment – "If anyone is moving back in, it's me" – that a tiny alarm began to sound from somewhere deep in her soul? It was unsettling and all she wanted to do was sit in the darkening living room alone and quiet to perhaps sort out some of the confusion.

"So, what do you want to do?"

His voice, confident, happy, his step lively and sure were all such a contradiction to her own melancholia, it was almost an insult. It wasn't his fault though. He knew nothing of her turmoil, and she mustn't blame him.

"Oh, I don't know. I have a casserole in the oven." As she spoke, she remembered the rich chocolate cake made earlier in the throes of her temper. "Oh yes and dessert – I hope you like chocolate."

"Oh yeah, I love it. My mum makes a brilliant chocolate pudding."

There it was again, the unconscious linking of her to his parent's generation. It struck her then, in the warm late afternoon that this was not going to work. This dream was ridiculous, and this love was hopeless. Although she did not believe it to be wrong or forbidden, it was impossible.

What was she to do now? She had invited him back to the house. He was expecting food and yes probably sex and she couldn't, she just couldn't. As they reached the front door, she pulled her bag from her shoulder to look for the key but before she pulled back the zip, he had taken a jangling bunch from his pocket and slid the key into the lock. He stepped into the house and pressed the buttons on the alarm. He threw his jacket onto the chair at the bottom of the stairs and walked through to the kitchen. He ran water into the kettle and then pulled open the oven door lifting the lid on the big metal casserole.

"Mmmm, that smells great. I'm starving."

A tiny nub of irritation joined the other negative emotions and suddenly it was all too much.

"Look, Jacob, I don't feel all that well to be honest."

He turned to look at her, his head cocked to one side, puzzlement creasing his forehead.

"Would you mind if I just went up to bed? My head is pounding and I just don't think I can face food right now."

"Oh, you poor thing. Hey, let me get you an aspirin." He took a glass and began to run water into it. "Let's get you up to bed." He handed her the bottle of pain killers that she kept in the kitchen cabinet and then wrapping his arm around her shoulders he ushered her towards the staircase.

"I'm sorry."

"No, don't worry, you can't help it."

"Look, why don't you take that casserole and the cake and share them with your friends, back at your house?"

"I wouldn't dream of it. I'll tell you what, I think I should stay, don't you? If you're not feeling very well you shouldn't be on your own."

"I'll be fine. It's only a headache really."

"No, I'll stay. I don't have lectures until tomorrow afternoon, I'll stay. I'll save you some of the casserole, will it be okay if I cut the cake though?"

This is not what she wanted, she wanted peace, solitude, her head didn't really ache but her heart did and she needed time to soothe it and to clear her thinking.

"I think really, Jacob, I would like to be on my own. I just want to sleep."

"Yeah, well I..." He looked into her eyes. "Oh, you're saying you want me to go?"

She couldn't speak but gave a twitch of her head.

"Oh right. Fine. Okay then."

He looked so very hurt, puzzled, and there at the back of his eyes did she see a flash of anger? No, no it was just the change in plan that had caught him unprepared.

"Right. Well, I hope you feel better soon." He bent and pecked her on the cheek as he reached for his jacket and stepped past her towards the door.

Chapter 31

As the light faded and the sounds of day segued into the more muted noises of the evening Mary sat in her living room lost in the maelstrom of her thoughts. She knew that what she had done, the loving, was never wrong, not in the way that Jane had insinuated; she still believed it had been pure and good. Then there was all the other "stuff". She could see now that the relationship was doomed, and it had been since the day Jacob had first taken her in his arms.

They should have stayed friends. Even if she had allowed him to come and live with her, it should have gone no further than that. If only she had been stronger and less ready to indulge her senses. If she had looked but not touched, admiring from a safe distance. Maybe she could have enjoyed his company now and again and even that of some of his friends. Now it was blighted, the sex had ruined everything. She knew there was no going back from that. It would be there at their every meeting, a frisson of energy in each touch, every glance, probably more for her than for him, but it would be there.

She couldn't be a part of his world and in truth she didn't think that she wanted to be. If he were to become part of hers then how would her friends and family regard him? Would they make the assumptions that Jane had made, and mistrust and dislike him? Perhaps, or maybe they would see him as the son that she never had, and how confused and betrayed would they feel then when they learned the truth? No, it had to end, and she wished that it was already over. If she never saw him again it would be possible to put this behind her, as a silly mistake. In time maybe it would become a warm memory, a little walk along a path that it had been unwise to tread. First though she had to end it and she didn't know how to do that and wasn't sure that she had the strength.

She closed her eyes, rested her head against the cushions and before long began to drift into a world that wasn't quite sleep but let herself go, soothed by the peace. When the doorbell rang, she was shocked upright in an instant, every nerve end jangling. She wasn't absolutely sure it had been the bell but it rang again. She stole to the bay window and peered around the corner from where she had a clear view of the front porch. Deep in her mind a hope that it was Jane had kicked at her but the figure standing in the orange light of the lamp, though a woman, was smaller and slight.

She put on the safety chain and unlocked the door, the anxious face in the semi darkness was only vaguely familiar but there was something she recognised.

"Hello, sorry to disturb you, Mary. It's me, it's Judy. We met today. I was in the pub, this afternoon."

"Oh Judy, hi. Jacob's not here. I had a headache and he went home."

"Sorry, I don't want to disturb you, I know he's not here. I'm Steve's girlfriend; I was at the house when he came back. Do you think I could come in, just for a minute?"

Mary didn't answer but slid the chain out of the catch and gave the young woman access to the hallway.

"I'm really sorry to come round like this. I wouldn't have done, if he'd still been here but I saw him at the house and – well anyway, here I am."

"Come in, come into the living room, do you want a drink? Some wine, a cup of tea?"

"That would be nice. Could I have a glass of water do you think? Just tap water's fine."

Mary put the glass on the table and then sat in a chair opposite the settee where Judy sat picking at her fingernails, her thin legs drummed jerkily, and she obviously felt nervous and out of place.

"What can I do for you Judy? Look, before we go any further, I think I should say that I don't take in lodgers," Mary said as she cocked her head, "if that's what you came about. It was just a temporary thing with Jacob, erm Jake."

"No, I'm not looking for anywhere; I've got a good place, a shared flat, no it's not that. I just, oh God I don't know how to put this."

She lifted the glass and sipped the water and then leaning forward to replace it on the table she took a deep breath, seemed to gather her resources and looked into Mary's face.

"Today in the pub, I thought that I detected something between you and Jake." Mary opened her mouth to speak but Judy stilled her with a raised hand and a shake of the head. "It's none of my business of course and it doesn't make any difference to me, not at all. You're a grown woman, and if I'm totally out of turn here then I'm sorry but all I want to say to you is be careful. I don't know how things are with you but if you and Jake have got a thing going on, if you have just – oh I don't know – be careful."

"I don't understand, what do you mean, careful, careful about what?"

"Just about how close you let him get, how much you - um I don't know how to say it. Look my friend went out with him, just for a little while and then she found him too needy, too dependent and she finished with him and...

well in the end she had to leave, had to go back home to her old place, her mum and dad's, she had to drop out and start again. He made it too difficult for her. I don't want to say any more. I shouldn't have come. It's none of my business."

With that she sprang to her feet and scurried for the front door. Mary chased after her.

"Wait, Judy, I don't know what you mean. Please come back, tell me what you mean, how did he make it difficult? Please won't you explain?"

With a shake of her head Judy slid through the door and almost running in her haste to get away, she disappeared down the street and out of sight around the corner. Mary could do nothing more than stand at her gatepost in the darkness watching.

Chapter 32

Had she loved him? Did she still, or had it all been a dream, just a step into madness? Now in the kitchen with a cup of tea cradled in her hands she tried to examine her feelings. She had never thought of herself as fickle, in the years of her marriage she had been stalwart and faithful. What had this been? Genuine deep feeling, a craziness caused by her hormones, a crush? She had needed Jacob. The thought of his touch had thrilled her and the simple sweep of his eyes across her face took her breath away. Yes, she had loved him, still did, but it was soured with all that had happened. Incredibly it had all gone so very badly wrong in just two short days and the man himself had done nothing wrong.

She sighed, it was all too difficult, and now this new thing, the visit by Judy, what on earth was behind all that? It was silly, schoolyard behaviour – *"My friend used to go out with your boyfriend"*. No, there could be nothing to it; young people were more prone to overreact and dramatize things.

She would ignore the visit, but what was impossible to ignore was this pressing need to sort everything out. She must break free, let him go. There was no help for it, though it hurt there was no future for them and it was better to end it now and to move on. She would draw back and leave him the opportunity to find love with a woman of his own age, one who would be comfortable in his sphere, one who would raise no eyebrows and who could go forward with him as she could not.

She realised also that there was the chance that she attached far more importance to the thing than he did. There had been no talk of permanence or of love. They had enjoyed some sex, laughed and talked together and been friends but now she realised that she didn't know how much it had meant to him. When she had been so distressed, after the argument with Jane, when she had hinted that she wouldn't see him again, he hadn't fought it – had he? He had simply told her to be sure of what she wanted. His reaction had been understated and calm but perhaps that was just because he was a man, although he hadn't let her go. It was so soon after that he had taken her to meet his friends, surely another step forward in a relationship. She shook her head. It was useless to go over it and over it, it was all too hard, and she was tired to the core. Tomorrow she would call him and tell him it was over.

The phone rang and the machine answered but then her mother's voice drifted through from the hall.

"Mary, Mary if you're there pick up, I need to speak to you. Are you there?"

"Hi mum. How are you, is something wrong?"

"No, well not really. That friend of yours, Jane, has been on the phone. Some story about you and a lodger. I told her not to be silly, that you wouldn't take a lodger, it was a misunderstanding. She said it was a young boy and – oh Mary she said some other things, awful things. I put the phone down on her but I had to ring, I had to let you know what she's doing. She said you were having an affair with him, this boy, that he was only twenty. What's the matter with her Mary? I thought she was your best friend.

Have you two had a row? You need to tell her not to spread such rumours. It's wicked."

Mary closed her eyes and sagged against the wall, more trouble, was it never going to end. She was caught in a nightmare. What had been a delight was now devastation.

Her mother's continued conversation was just so much white noise, the world swam and for a moment it seemed that she would faint. She fell back on the excuse she had used earlier in the day.

"Look Mum, I'm sorry I've got a rotten headache, can I speak to you later? I'll call you tomorrow, in the evening."

"Oh, well alright, take some aspirin. I just thought I'd let you know what was going on. It upset me, you know? Anyway, I'll speak to you tomorrow, when you get home from work."

"Yes, okay Mum, don't worry, there's nothing to be upset about."

She pressed the off button and slid to the floor to sit with her head buried between her bent knees. What had happened? How had her quiet, ordered world become this disaster? On top of everything else she had now been reminded that tomorrow it was time to return to work and behave as if all was well.

Moving like an old woman she pushed to her feet and banister-dragged herself up the stairs. She passed the guest room and caught sight of the bed, the duvet wrinkled, and the pillow-cases creased where their heads had lain, and with a great sob she reached out and dragged the door closed. She staggered to her own room and threw off the jeans and sweater chosen with such care just a few hours ago. In the drawer was a box of sleeping pills, prescribed in the days after Bill died, they were almost certainly out of date but she swallowed two down anyway. She lay on her back in the darkness, tears trickled across her face to dampen the bedding as she waited for the chemicals to rescue her from the drama that life had become.

Chapter 33

It was difficult climbing back to reality. It was dark where she was and there was an urgent need to escape. Struggling and pushing against the effects of the sleeping tablets Mary dragged her way free of the fug. They had always knocked her for six and that was why there were so many now in the little box. She didn't like them, didn't enjoy the loss of control and especially disliked the horrible dulling of her senses for hours the next morning.

She shifted under the cover. Last night the drapes had remained open and the sun was streaming through the net curtain. She could feel it warm where it touched her bare arm. Hmm, nice. The birds were busy in the tree outside the window and a sense of peace wrapped her around briefly. Then it all came back, bits and pieces, knocks and bumps. The need to see Jacob and tell him what she had decided. A day at work stretching before her when she would need to be bright and helpful to the patients and friendly to her colleagues and last of all the phone call to her mother and the drama that would be unleashed with that. As her spirits sank, she dragged the duvet over her head and hid in the warm darkness.

The noise didn't register at first. Her hearing was muted by the down of the bedcovers and her senses deadened by the effect of the pills but eventually it occurred to her that something was going on that shouldn't be.

She poked her face over the top of the cotton cover, water was running. She glanced out of the window, and a bright warm morning smiled back at her. No rain. She leapt from the bed, there must be a leak. Her bare feet shushed across the carpet as she hurried out onto the landing. The sound was coming from the guest room. That door was closed last night surely. She remembered the assault that the rumpled bed had made on her rattled nerves and recalled distinctly shutting off the sight of it on the way to her own room. Now the door was ajar, the smell of soap drifted to her and the sound of the shower dispelled any further worry of a leak. She took a step forward and raised her hand. As the door fell back, she could make out on the chair by the window a pair of jeans, a sweatshirt and there was a small sports bag on the end of the bed. She gulped, already on one level she knew what this was but still a frisson of fear caused her breathing to quicken and her stomach to curl into a tight ball.

She stepped fully into the room and through the partly closed bathroom door she could see Jacob. His back was to her, soapy water tracking down across the pink skin of his shoulders and running across his behind. She scuttled again onto the landing where she stood for a moment holding the door frame for support and fought with her befuddled memory of the day before. Did she know he was here? Had she, in the drug-induced sleep of last night forgotten that he was sleeping in her guest room? No, she had not. He was not supposed to be here. She had sent him home yesterday with the excuse of her headache and had not spoken to him since. Apart from that Judy, during the strange visit, had said she had seen him at his own house. Why then, what possible reason could there be for him to be here now in her home?

She dragged on her dressing gown and checked the time. She made her way to the kitchen and filled the kettle. Her tumbled thoughts demanded attention but it was impossible to straighten them into any sort of order. Working on instinct she popped tea bags into two mugs, and set two places at the table. At the little table she lowered her face into her hands. Her head was foggy, her mouth was dry with the effects of the pills and her senses were zinging with alarm; this was wrong and unsettling.

As his feet thundered on the stairs, she raised her head.

"Morning, Lovely lady."

"Jacob, I didn't know you were here." It was ludicrous but no other words found their way out of her mouth.

"No, well. The thing is there was a party at the house. God it was noisy and so I thought I'd sleep here."

"But, when did you arrive?"

"It was late, not that late but you'd already gone to bed of course, with your poor head. Are you feeling better?"

"Yes, thanks, but Jacob, you just let yourself in?"

"Well I didn't want to disturb you, with you not feeling well so yes, I used my key. Is the tea ready, hey have we got any bacon?"

Chapter 34

"Do you want more tea?" Jacob held up the kettle and turned from the sink.

"No, I haven't time. I need to get to work."

"But you haven't eaten anything. Aw, you poor thing have you still got a headache?"

As he leaned down to wrap his arm around her shoulder Mary stiffened. Tears were a tiny beat away. She couldn't deal with this now. There wasn't time, she was never, ever late for work and anyway she didn't know what to say, how to react. She was in truth a little afraid, and a quiver of panic fluttered in her chest. She felt control slipping away, her home and her life being invaded.

When he had first come to share her space Mary had been thrilled, happy, but there was something so very unsettling about the way he had used her house, entered while she was sleeping and was now clattering around the kitchen making his breakfast, turning on the radio when all she needed was peace and silence. She pushed away from the table and ran up the stairs to her room. With quivering fingers, she applied a hint of makeup and dragged on her uniform.

It would all have to wait. She must step now into work mode and concentrate on her duties. She picked up her bag and turned into the kitchen.

"I'm going now, Jacob. You'll leave the place tidy, will you?"

"Yes, of course I will. Hey, you don't look too good, are you sure you're well enough to go to work? Maybe you're coming down with something."

"I'm fine, really."

"Oh, okay. I won't be in tonight when you get back. I have some stuff to do and then some of us are going to the gym. I'm not sure where I'll sleep though. So, I might see you later, right?"

Though the clock was taunting her she couldn't simply walk away from this. "I thought you had moved out, Jacob. I mean, I wasn't expecting that you'd be coming back, like this I mean."

"Aw come on now, you must have known that I couldn't just leave you. I mean I need to see you, don't I? And I thought you wanted to see me. You do still want to see me, don't you?"

His face had clouded with puzzlement. It was impossible to handle this now. There wasn't time and so she would have to leave for the surgery feeling confused and anxious.

"I think we need to have a chat, you know, about where we go from here but I'm in a hurry now. I'll speak to you tonight."

Jacob strode across the kitchen and wrapped her in his arms.

"Oh, poor Mary you are out of sorts, aren't you? Look, I'll make a point of getting back early tonight. We can sit and have a nice drink and I'll get us a curry, or maybe a pizza and we can just have a night in, the two of us. I've been insensitive, haven't I? You're still upset about Jane and I didn't realise, I'm sorry."

"No, it's not that – well yes, it is. Oh Jacob, yes of course I'm upset about Jane but there's more to it than that and I need for us to have a talk and sort things out."

He kissed the top of her head.

"Look, you're not well and this is not the time for all this. We'll talk tonight. I'll try not to be late – okay?"

There was no choice but to nod her head, and so Mary grabbed her keys and dashed from the house out of her depth and knocked off balance. For the first time that she could ever remember she dreaded the day at work and the long hours until she could give this problem the time and consideration that it needed. She buckled herself into the little car and turned into the road.

Chapter 35

She could smell cooking even before she eased herself out of the car. Mary had struggled through the day. Keeping busy and throwing herself into work had helped. Whenever the stack of her own problems threatened to bury her, she found something else to do, another task to occupy her hands and mind. Once on the journey home though all the problems swarmed in and wouldn't be beaten back.

So, she would work through the list calmly. First, she would make the call to her mum. What tone that would take was yet to be decided. It was essential to convince her that there was no need for worry otherwise there would be phone calls every day and visits and drama. It would be suffocating and difficult. She knew that her parents meant well but since Bill died, they seemed to have felt the need to slot back into the place they occupied before she was married. Gradually over time things had improved but it didn't take much, a dose of flu or a breakdown with the car, and they were back fussing and advising.

The situation that she was in now was so far outside anything that she could ever discuss with them that it was vital that their worries were allayed, and quickly. She couldn't lie but there must be a way to convince them that all was well. She sighed because of course all was not well, all was very far from well. Tension and stress wore her out and right now she was completely drained.

The rich smell of roasting meat was wonderful. She felt a pang of envy for the family next door who would be sitting down to dinner together, all normal and calm in their world. As she unlocked her own door it was obvious though that someone was cooking in her kitchen.

Of course it would be Jacob. She hung her coat in the cupboard under the stairs and leaned around the kitchen doorway. The table was laid, a vase of flowers was in the centre and a bottle of red wine stood opened to breathe beside them. Jacob turned.

"Hi, there. Roast chicken, I hope that's okay. Oh, you look better, that's brilliant."

He crossed the room and threw his arms around her. She raised her face to his and he kissed her deeply on the lips. There was no other choice but to submit, his lips warm and soft on hers and his firm arms felt so very good.

"I thought you were going to the gym?"

"Well I was but you looked so very sad and unwell this morning I thought that it would be far better for me to look after my favourite lady than my abs." He grinned down at her. "Here let me pour you some wine and you sit down here and talk to me while I finish scraping the carrots."

He bustled back and forth checking the oven, shuffling pans and warming plates and as she sipped at the glass of red Mary felt the tension leave her shoulders and neck and her insides untied themselves for the first time for days. "You're good at this Jacob, I hadn't realised."

"Yes, well my mum insisted, 'Just because you're a boy,' she used to say, 'it doesn't mean you shouldn't be able to look after yourself properly'."

"Well she did a good job."

"Huh, yes with me and my brother but Lyndsey can't boil an egg without burning it, mind you that's not totally Mum's fault. Lyndsey's very bright and just hasn't got room for ordinary everyday things like eating." He grinned at her.

"Were you happy at home?"

He stopped his busyness and turned to her.

"It was okay, there were some problems now and again. I suppose all families have things. It's never all sweetness and light, is it?"

"Oh, I'm sorry, I shouldn't have asked. I didn't mean to pry."

"No, it's fine. Mostly it's okay now, now I'm away, you know."

She let it drop. He served up the meal and they clicked back into the easiness of the previous weeks. The wine and warmth and his kind attention soothed the edges and hid the worries and, tired as she was, Mary let them drift away. As they were deciding whether or not they wanted coffee the phone rang. She let the machine answer and her mother's voice drifted through and inveigled itself into the relaxed atmosphere of the kitchen.

"Mary, you didn't ring me. I've been waiting. I've even missed my programme waiting for you to call. I do need you to tell me what's been going on with that Jane and all this talk of you having a toy boy. Mary, are you there, Mary?"

She felt the heat in her cheeks and the sickness back in her gut as she raised her eyes to his and saw the question in his face, and behind the puzzlement again, that flash of annoyance.

Chapter 36

Trapped by a flush of indecision Mary glanced into the hall. Her mother had obviously replaced the phone after leaving her rather hysterical message. She turned to find Jacob, eyes lowered playing with the edge of the paper napkin.

Thoughts tumbled and rolled through her mind. Would it be best to make a joke now or perhaps simply tut and leave it? Words refused to collect in any sort of order. "Jacob." That was it, just his name and he didn't respond. "I…" It was hopeless, so she gave up.

Now he shifted on the chair, raised his eyes to hers. She couldn't read his expression. Was he upset, amused, or was he angry? Impossible to tell.

The moments ticked by, she wanted to take some action to break the silence and move things along. The happy mood was lost. She couldn't make out what had replaced it but there was a threat in the air, something unfathomable and deeply uncomfortable. As she tensed her fingers on the tabletop ready to push the chair back, he laid his hand on top of hers.

"Toy boy?"

"Not my words Jacob, never my words. I haven't spoken to my mum about you, not at all. Jane called her and poked her nose into my business and my mum has overreacted. I haven't said anything to anyone about us, well not about how we are, how we've been, you know."

"How have we been Mary? Tell me, in your opinion, how have we been?"

"Well, you know the erm, the sex and the closeness, all of that."

"You know everything was alright before you told Jane about us. It was lovely. I thought you were happy, and we were good together."

"Yes, we were, it was lovely. It really was, and I didn't mean to tell Jane. It just came out. I never meant to talk about you to her but well, I suppose I just wanted to share how I felt with my friend. Anyway, I see now it was silly."

"Is it still lovely, Mary? Do you still think it's good?"

"Well, I was upset you know, with Jane's reaction."

"Yes, but what do you think? Do you think it's still lovely?" His face had hardened and the grip on her hand was tight, painful. She fought back a flicker of fear and took a deep breath.

"I like you such a lot Jacob. I have done since the first time we met, that silly day in the road." She tried to drag her hand away but he moved his own to trap it more firmly against the tabletop. The delicate bones of her fingers ground under his grip. "I didn't expect this thing to happen and I was so happy, I couldn't believe it but then…"

He tipped his head to one side, narrowed his eyes but didn't speak. She needed him to speak, the better to read his mood and judge how to continue. She couldn't remember ever feeling so physically threatened. It was a gut instinct fed by his stillness, the dead stare of his eyes and the pain of his grip on her hand. From somewhere she summoned up bravery to speak honestly to him.

"I think maybe Jacob I have made a mistake, well that we both have. I didn't think enough about the differences between us, the age thing of course but really everything. I was swept along and lost control. We are in such different places in our lives, aren't we? You are so young. You have such a lot of stuff still to do. I don't think I'm right for you just now. This relationship, maybe it'll hold you back you know, stop you doing things you should be doing. I didn't feel so comfortable with your friends the other day. I felt old and I was worried about what they would think of me, if they knew and – oh Jacob, I just think maybe this is wrong, for you, for us."

She shook her head as she finished speaking and tried again to pull her hand away. The tension in her muscles was screaming and panic was creeping in.

His face creased with anguish and great tears ballooned on the bottom lids of his eyes ready to overflow and run across his cheeks.

"I thought you liked me, Mary. I really thought you did. I thought you were different, genuine. You in your pretty blouses with your shining hair, your sweetness, but now I see I'm just a joke to you, fuel for gossip, a toy boy!"

"No, no, I told you I never said that, they weren't my words."

As he raised his hand to brush away the moisture on his face she leapt up from the table. Her instinct was to go to him, to wrap her arms around him and rock him like the child she had never had. Her heart urged her to comfort him but, the tension of the last few minutes, the violence that pulsed in the air between them held her back and she stood looking down at him as he angrily dried his cheek.

"You're all the same, aren't you? Always the same, gossiping and twittering like caged budgies. Talking behind our backs and laughing at us. I thought you were different. I thought you were nicer but you're not. You, you Mary, you're just the same as all the others."

The outburst was shocking. She raised a hand to still the words, to quiet the escalating level of his voice. His face was flushed with fury, his nostrils flaring. She stepped around the table and held out her arms palms upwards, entreating, begging for peace.

"Jacob, there's no need for you to be upset. I told you, I didn't mean to talk about you but I shared my thoughts with my friend."

"Why, why? I thought I was your friend. You care more about bloody Jane than you do about me. I thought what we had, what we did was special and now I find that you're just like all the rest. Like my mother, Lyndsey, all of you."

She didn't understand where the fury had come from and was shocked and afraid, and out of her depth in the face of such passion. As she leaned to him, he raised his hand, she saw the threat but didn't believe it. The possibility of physical attack was ludicrous, so far off her radar that she continued to approach him. He flung his arm towards her, the power of his shoulders behind the swipe and as his hand connected with her cheek she was flung sideways away from him to collide with the kitchen cabinet which struck her at the waist winding her and sending her into a heap on the tiles.

"See, see what you did, see what you did? Are you happy now that you made me do that? Mary, how could you?"

Before she had time to catch her breath and fully register the enormity of what had happened, he stalked across the tiles and dragged her to her feet. His hand moved to her head, fisting in her hair and pulling her face towards his. She thought that he would kiss her and closed her eyes. Instead he hissed at her.

"You let me down. You are a disappointment, that's what you are."

Before she had a chance to speak or squirm from his grasp, he lashed out again backhanding her across the face.

Her ears rang and flashes of light exploded behind her eyes and then suddenly it was over. He released his grip on her hair and let her drop to the floor where she sat sobbing in confusion. He swung away and grabbed his jacket and backpack storming from the room which descended into surreal quiet, the clock ticking happily and the kettle beginning to hum.

Afterwards when she tried to replay what had happened her brain refused to form the pictures. As she sat on the settee with a cold cloth on her face to reduce the swelling and to minimise any bruising, she was unable to piece it together. All she could remember was the sudden yelling, the sound of his hand as it swiped at her face and the scream that seemed to come from somewhere far away but which left her throat raw.

Chapter 37

She locked the door and put on the safety chain, set the alarm and then creaked up the stairs. The hot water in the shower hid her tears and in truth she didn't know when the crying started but stepping out into the steamy bathroom, she was wracked with great shuddering sobs. She wouldn't be going to work in the morning, not with the marks on her face. She had worked at the surgery for a long time and she had seen the cowed and frightened wives and girlfriends and heard the excuses; cupboard doors, and inexplicably unseen obstacles, bruising and cutting tender flesh. She had heard some of the tales and read the reports and she was not going down that road.

No matter what happened there would be no lying, or making excuses. She didn't want to go to the police. She could see how it would look – an older woman, lonely and desperate for attention and a young man driven by passion and hormones. Oh, she had no doubt they would pay lip service, be polite, probably send an officer around to comfort and cajole and lead her to a court hearing but she wouldn't do it. Right now, at this hour she didn't know what she was going to do. The shock and the pain had deadened her brain and she was drifting in a strange place unable to think clearly.

She climbed under the covers and wrapped herself in the scent of fabric softener and sanity. Quietly in the darkness she lay with eyes closed fighting back the fears and the anguish, waiting for dawn. Eventually she slept.

The sounds of the street woke her. For a moment the unfamiliar feel of her face, eye swollen shut, and soreness on her lips and cheekbone was puzzling and then it swept back and she knew there were things to do, and quickly. She called the surgery and told them she was ill and asked for permission to take some holiday time. They were put out and sniffy but there was nothing she could do. Maybe eventually she would tell them the truth, the colleagues that could be trusted, but for now the lie was almost the truth and it had to suffice.

She threw some clothes into a bag whilst routinely looking through the window in the living room. When the gate rattled, she scuttled into the corner to hide until it was clear it was only the postman.

She was afraid. She was afraid that if he came back and found her, that he would be violent again or maybe he wouldn't. Maybe he would be tearful and bereft. If he came and told her he was sorry, that it was a moment of madness, that he didn't know why he had done it, she knew her fear would compel her tell him that it was all alright, that she forgave him. But it wasn't alright, not at all and she would not forgive him ever, and to give voice to such a thought would be unbearable.

She would have to go away until she could make her world safe again. Right now, she wasn't sure how to do it, but the first thing was to flee.

The small black travel bag sat on the landing and her soft wool coat wrapped around her like a friend. Mary stepped back into the bedroom for a last glance to make sure that nothing of importance had been overlooked and her eye settled on the framed photograph of Bill sitting on the dresser. She crossed the floor to lift the small frame and stroke the image with a quivering finger.

"What are you doing?" She heard him deep inside her ears, she heard her husband not as a ghostly whisper but as a vivid memory. Quiet and kind as he had been even when he was riven by the illness and made short-tempered by the pain, he had never turned on her, never been anything but gentle. "What are you thinking?"

Right now the need to speak to her husband and to have him hold her hand was a physical ache. They had moved into the little house about ten years before the start of his illness and they had loved it. They had decorated and improved it together and when the time came for him to die, he had come home to their place. What would he think if he saw her now preparing to run away and leave it when they had faced so very much here? Bill had been brave and taken strength from the love within the walls. Surely, she should do that now. Facing this awful thing, why would she run?

Her eyes swept around the bright bedroom. This was her home, her haven. The things that rested in this room had meaning to her and still resonated with Bill's touch. She didn't want to leave, or to have to sleep in some cold hotel and eat her meals in cafés and bars. She wanted to be here, here with the things that she loved. The new-found resolve that swept her body was now absolute. She had made a mistake. Jane had been right in some of what she had said. She felt herself a fool but did not want to be a coward as well. No, she would stay and face what had happened and would act, and though it would be impossible to obliterate the violence, after all the blow had fallen quite literally, now was not a time to run and hide, now was a time to fight back and to balance the scales.

She took out her digital camera and recorded photographs of her ruined face from each angle that she could manage. She shrugged off her coat and moved the bag back into the room, she would unpack later. Running to the computer she downloaded the images and saved them both on the hard drive and then on a memory stick which she placed in the very back of her desk drawer.

The plan that was forming was still a wisp in the ether but the need to put things right was strong. She went back upstairs and experimented a little with her make-up. She would need to go out later, and though she couldn't hide the bruise totally she thought that she could lessen it enough so that it wouldn't be so visible in the dimness of her car. Turning back to the picture of Bill, she kissed the end of her finger before stroking it gently against the glass. She would regain her pride and her self-respect and no violent, selfish boy would drive her from her home.

Chapter 38

The kitchen was in disarray. As the kettle boiled, she loaded the dishwasher and wiped the surfaces. Sunshine winked on the reflective points and the morning was bright, but as she glanced at the chairs tumbled away from the table and the dried food still smeared on spoons and pans, the whole nasty episode flooded back. She straightened her back and took in a deep breath. She had made a terrible error of judgement but was not the guilty party. What Jacob had done was wicked and such violence could never be justified. She wasn't a vengeful person and didn't normally hold a grudge but she had never before been the victim of physical violence and it had unlocked in her something powerful and undeniable.

She glanced at the kitchen clock and was stunned to find that the morning was almost gone. The first part of her plan needed her to be outside the college when they broke for lunch and if she didn't leave within the next few minutes it would be too late. As she made her way to the coat cupboard the phone rang and with a sinking heart, she heard her mother's voice over the answering machine.

"Mary, what is going on? You didn't call back and when I rang your work this morning, they said that you were sick. Dad and I are coming down this afternoon. This is not like you, I'm quite upset."

No, they mustn't come, they mustn't see her bruised and swollen face. They wouldn't be put off with an invented story of a fall but would want to know every detail and nuance and she knew that it would be impossible to weave a convincing tale. She leapt forward and snatched up the receiver.

"Mum, hi. Sorry I didn't get back to you. To be honest that headache really was awful and it turned into a migraine."

"I didn't know you had migraines."

"Well no, no I don't, not normally but oh you know. I rang NHS direct and they reckon it could be the menopause. Anyway, I'm going to take a few days off work and then when I'm back I'll have a word with Doctor Ormerod."

"Oh, well okay. Are you alright now though? It's not like you to take time off work."

"Yes, I'm fine but I'm tired you know and I thought well, rather than take sick leave I'd just take some of my holiday."

"Well, why don't I come down and we can go out for a look around the shops and have a bite to eat, would you like that?"

"No, no. Maybe in a day or two." She glanced around desperately, this was getting out of hand and the more it went on, the deeper she would dig.

"Oh blimey, Mum. I'm going to have to go. I left the tap running. I'll call you, don't bother coming down though, really there's no need and I'd rather have a trip out when I'm completely better."

"Oh, well yes, go on, run. I'll call you again this evening."

"Great."

She hung up the phone and stood for a moment trying to clear her mind. Now she felt guilty. Mum and Dad meant well, and they in their turn had done nothing but care about her. Now, because of her involvement with Jacob, she was lying and trying to avoid them. She shook her head in disbelief. Life had become so complicated so very quickly. A throb started over her eyes and a genuine headache threatened. She took a couple of aspirins and checked the time again. Maybe if she hurried, she could still make it.

She raised a hand to slide the chain from the little catch and the next thought struck like a blow.

He had a key.

Jacob had a key and if she left the house now there was no guarantee that he wouldn't let himself in to wait for her. She was trapped. He had imprisoned her in her own home. Now she slid the safety chain back in place and turned the deadlock. Tears sprang to her eyes as she took a couple of backward paces to lower herself onto the bottom stair and hide her face in her hands. His influence was creeping into every part of her life now and this thing that had started as such a thrill, was a black monster threatening to destroy all that she held dear.

Chapter 39

The locks would have to be changed. The one on the back door was probably okay but the two on the front must be done quickly. She dragged out the Yellow Pages and looked for an emergency number.

"Hello, Marsden Locksmiths. Can I help you?"

"Yes, I need a new lock on my front door. Someone has a key. Sorry, what I mean is someone I don't want to come in has a key."

"Okay, do you know what sort of lock it is, madam?"

"One is a Yale I know that, with extra levers I think you call them, and then there is a mortice. Does that make sense?"

"I'll tell you what, why don't I send one of our locksmiths round to have a look? He'll have some replacement parts with him but if he needs anything else, we carry a very extensive stock. How urgent is it?"

"It's urgent. There is someone out there with a key and I don't want him being able to get in at all. I can't go out unless I know the house is secure and I have to keep the chain on while I'm here."

"I'll send Barry round. He should be with you by three o'clock, is that okay?"

"Three o'clock, oh not sooner?"

"Well, not really that's about the best I can do. If you are in danger your best bet really would be to call the police."

"Yes, of course, sorry it's just such a worry. I'll be fine thanks. Yes, three o'clock will be great."

"I'll ask him to get to you as soon as he can, just let me make note of your address."

"Thanks, I appreciate that." She recited the address and replaced the handset.

So, the plan had been thwarted before the first step but she could use the time to clarify her thoughts. Delay was bad. If momentum was lost there was a real danger that she would lose her nerve, plus it was essential to find Judy while her face was still obviously raw and sore.

The mobile buzzed on the tabletop and burst into its happy little jingle. She snatched it up and drew in a sharp breath. It was Jacob. Obviously, she wasn't going to answer it and after a dozen rings it cut off. She didn't use the message service so his attempt at contact would come to nothing. She sat looking at her phone.

Her landline was ex-directory but did he have the number? She wasn't sure and the next few minutes were spent pleading silently for it to stay dumb. It did and so maybe that wasn't going to be a problem. She didn't want him able to leave messages but the answering machine was her way of filtering calls and she didn't want to disable it. Yet again he was interfering in her life, worming into the simplest of things.

Maybe she should call the police after all. If she did contact them now, while her face was still swollen and sore and the proof of his violence obvious, perhaps they would be able to stop him trying to contact her.

It was tempting to bring someone professional in but it would be unbearable. They may want her to have medical intervention and need a statement, perhaps they'd make her go to the police station. If she went down that road the whole nasty incident would be pretty much public knowledge and she didn't think she could stand it. People at work would know, her friends, her parents and the rest. They would gossip and offer opinions and advice and she just couldn't face it. After the incident with Jane she was determined that her private life would be just that until the culmination of her plan, and she knew then everything would be laid bare but hoped the satisfaction of a sort of justice would make it worthwhile.

Chapter 40

Three times he tried to call her and three times she sat staring at the glowing screen for a few brief seconds before pressing the reject call button, determined not to speak to him. She should have turned the phone off but locked into the house the way she was, it felt like a lifeline. Yes, she still had the landline but felt nervous and vulnerable and needed this extra contact with the outside world.

At just after two the doorbell rang and she scurried to the bay window in the living room. There was a blue van parked at the roadside and a young man in overalls standing on the step. He had turned away from the house to gaze vaguely at the garden. She could see his face clearly. This must be Barry.

"Hi, come in." He was holding an I.D. card out to her and she took it from his outstretched hand.

"I'm Barry. You been mugged then?"

Her hand flew to her face. "Oh."

"Sorry, but it looks pretty bad, bet that's sore. Don't worry though, I've seen worse. Lots of our customers have been mugged and when the office said it was urgent, I guessed it was something like that. Buggers they are, should be left on a deserted island the lot of 'em."

She stood back to let him in. He posed no threat and yet his very presence unnerved her. She didn't correct his assumptions; it was easier to say nothing than to weave a complicated explanation.

He stepped into the hallway, turned and began to examine the locks on her front entrance door.

"Oh yeah, I can do this no problem. Do you want me to get on with it straight away or do you want an estimate?"

"Please, just do it now, it's fine. I have to have it done. I have to know he can't get in." The locksmith turned and smiled at her.

"If you give me the police crime number, we can send the bill straight to the insurance company," Barry said. "You just have to try and put it behind you love. My gran was mugged, last year it was, but she's tough. First of all she ripped the bugger's jacket, still got away though but she said to me 'Barry, no scum like that is going to spoil my enjoyment of life', and she just put it behind her and got on with stuff. Yup, that's what you have to do.

"I'll be about an hour doing this. Do you need anything else seeing to? Windows, back gates, anything like that?"

"No, just this. He only has the key to this lock. I don't have a number, not from the police. I'll pay for it myself. If you give me a bill, I can give you a cheque or if you have a card reader…"

"I hope you've told the police. You have reported this, haven't you? You really have to. I know they don't do much but you should still tell 'em. Still it's your business love. Look you go and sit yourself somewhere nice and comfy and I'll let you know when I'm done."

"Thank you, Barry."

She sat on the settee listening to the small sounds as the locks were removed and new ones fitted. Barry hummed quietly to himself as he worked, and she allowed herself to relax. The warmth in the room and the nervous exhaustion combined to lull her into a half dream and she let her head fall against the chair back. The sound of the front gate didn't register as any sort of threat, it didn't really register at all, and it wasn't until she heard the sound of voices that she realised there was danger.

"Hello mate."

"Hello, can I just squeeze in there?" It was him. She had dreaded this, that he might come back unannounced and to arrive now, just when the door was without a lock and she had no way to bar his entrance. She leapt from the seat and ran to the living room door.

"Barry don't let him in, please, stop him. Don't let him come in."

A ludicrous frozen tableau formed. Barry, mouth gaping and screwdriver poised over the newly fitted lock had turned and behind him, one foot on the step the other still on the driveway, Jacob was staring at her. A great bunch of roses were clasped in front of him and a useless key dangled from his other hand.

"Keep him out, please Barry, keep him away from me."

Chapter 41

The brief hiatus was followed by chaos. Barry was spurred into action by the desperation in Mary's voice and with a hefty thrust he swung the door closed just as Jacob had begun to step across the threshold. The yell from the other side of the wood witnessed the jarring to his foot and the blow on the hand that he had raised to push his way forward.

"Shit, sorry, sorry." Barry was not a violent man and the yell from outside unnerved him.

"No, don't open the door. Keep him out please." Mary had run forward and was now standing beside the locksmith and leaning against the door. "Is it locked, did the new lock work?"

"It's latched love, hey calm down, it's okay."

"Can you lock it, make it safe?" In response Barry simply flicked the little gold knob.

"There y'are love. He hasn't got a key anyway." He jingled a tiny bunch of keys and handed them forward to Mary who took them in quivering fingers. Jacob now began hammering on the door.

"Mary, I need to speak to you. We should talk. I really need to come in. Come on Mary, open the door."

Barry's head swung back and forth, his eyes wide in confusion.

"What are ya gonna do, love? He had flowers for you."

"Yes, I know but he can't come in. I don't want him in here."

Realisation dawned then and Barry shook his head.

"Bloody hell. So he did that?"

He pointed at the bruises on Mary's cheek now a livid red and blue and at her bloodshot eye which was still swollen and puffy. In response she simply nodded.

"I bet you haven't been to the police, have you? This is why you didn't want the insurance company involved."

There was genuine sympathy in his eyes and Mary thought she would cry in the face of his kindness. She swallowed hard.

"I can't get in touch with the police, I couldn't bear it. I know you're right but I just can't."

Barry reached out and touched her arm.

"Don't get upset love, it's nothing to do with me. You have to do what you have to do. Anyway, listen I think he's gone. You stay here and I'll go and look out through the window." He strode through to the living room and shouted back to her, "Yes he's off down the street now. He's flung them flowers in the road and he's storming off. My God love he looks as though he has a temper on him and no mistake."

Mary had joined him in the quiet room. She was shaking and the tears had refused to be held back, she swiped them away impatiently.

"Oh look, don't be upset. Shall I make you a cup of tea? That's what you need, a nice cup of tea, settle you down."

"Will you have one with me?" Mary asked.

Barry glanced at his wristwatch.

"Oh well okay, why not. I'll put the kettle on, you stay here, sit down and try to get yourself together."

She sat on the chair lost in confusion while a stranger clattered about in her kitchen searching for cups and spoons. He came back bringing mugs of tea and even a plate of biscuits. He smiled at her as he lowered the tray to the coffee table.

"Are you feeling a bit better?"

Mary dredged up a grin and nodded.

"Thank you, Barry, I am really grateful. I'm so embarrassed and sorry that you got involved in that but I'm glad you were here. Thank you."

He blushed and hid his awkwardness by handing her one of the cups and taking his own with him as he went back to the window.

"Well he's long gone now, I think. You're probably going to have to do something about it all though aren't you? I mean it's not going to just go away. Was he living here then? Sorry, none of my business."

He gulped back his drink, obviously desperate to escape this difficult situation.

"If I was you, I'd be calling the police I would, but I expect it's tricky under the circumstances. I'll get the office to send you a bill, you don't want to be messing about with cheques and stuff now. Are you going to be okay? On your own I mean?"

She nodded at him, overcome with shame and embarrassment now that the terror had dissipated.

"I'll be fine, thank you. I have to go out in a little while anyway but in the meantime, I have a safe door now thanks to you."

"Aye well, that's only a part of it, isn't it love? At the end of the day you will have to get together with him, your son, and sort things out. There are counselling places and so on you know. He needs help no doubt about it. Anyone who could do something like that to his mum needs help for certain."

She couldn't speak but simply watched as he collected his tools and replaced the mug on the tray. There were no words to form an answer to this assumption. She was humiliated and didn't trust herself to do anything other than simply walk behind Barry as he let himself out into the sunny afternoon and, at his urging, to lock and bolt the door.

Chapter 42

Over and over the phone rang, text after text landed with a sharp little chime. Mary ignored the calls and deleted the texts quickly. Of course, the first line scrolled across the little screen, *Mary why are you doing this – Mary we need to talk – Come on lovely lady don't be silly,* and so it went on. When she could stand it no longer, she turned it off. She would have to change her number; would it be possible to do it without buying a new phone? It was another complication and yet another intrusion and would mean that all her friends and family would need to be contacted but it was impossible to live with this continuous barracking.

It was a bright summer day. The sunglasses wouldn't look out of place and the sun hat with a floppy brim made her feel better about venturing out, though the bruising still showed on her cheek and chin. Perhaps anyone who saw her would think that she was a car crash victim or had fallen. Perhaps they just wouldn't care; the thought strangely gave her some comfort. She dressed herself with infinite care. In her mind a battered woman would not be smartly attired in well-cut trousers and expensive blouse but of course in her heart she knew this wasn't true, but it helped to bolster her flagging spirits and present a brave and respectable face to the world.

It was much later than she had planned and the college would now be finishing the day courses, or so she believed. It was such a long shot. First of all, she didn't know whether Judy would even be there today. She also had no way of knowing when Judy's lectures would be that day, though the course was to do with computer programming and so would probably take place in the IT building. The IT centre was nearer than the main college and thankfully not close to the Media centre which was housed in a converted theatre.

The streets around the college were thronged with students and Mary parked at the kerb alongside the cars of parents and taxis waiting for their passengers. She was thankful of the congestion and overcrowding which normally was a trial to anyone needing to visit the town centre. She felt anonymous and inconspicuous, exactly what she wanted, but the task itself was terribly difficult. She hadn't realised just how many people there would be, streams of them poured from the gates and meandered in all directions. Jeans, T shirts, a few pairs of shorts and every now and again a bright summer dress. It wasn't long before she realised the chance of actually spotting her quarry amongst so many young people, was minimal.

The only other option was one that sent a shiver of apprehension through her; she could go and park near the shared accommodation where Jacob lived. Judy was Steve's girlfriend and so perhaps she would be there with him. Mary felt disheartened and tired. This was ridiculous, the plan was so very complicated anyway and even to complete the first stage was proving far more difficult than she had anticipated. The wait for the locksmith had caused such a delay and all that happened after that had left her feeling mentally bruised. She would go home, and just try to put this behind her. She glanced into the rear-view mirror and her damaged face mocked her. *So he gets away*

No, that's not right.

She would keep going a little longer, go to the house and try to spot Judy and if that didn't work out then she didn't know what she would do. Perhaps at the end of the day the best thing would really be to let it all go. What would happen though if she met him again, in town, at the surgery or in the street? What if he came back to her home, hammered on the door and followed her in the road? He could make her life unliveable and she owed it to herself to take some action at least, something so that in the future when she replayed this horrible part of her life she wouldn't be shamed by her actions. She knew the importance of memories from the time after Bill's illness when she had dwelt with something approaching obsession on events that at the time had seemed small, perceived injustices, tiny misjudgements but also the comfort she took from the many kindnesses that they had shown each other in the progression through the darkness.

She had a plan of a sort, and she thought she knew who could help her. If it worked it could drive him away and give her back her peace and freedom.

The little car pulled into the traffic and headed towards the shared house.

Chapter 43

It was quiet in the suburban street. Mary parked her car around the corner. She walked gingerly back and spotted a bus shelter from where it seemed she would be able to observe activity without causing suspicion. She felt absolutely ridiculous. Wearing sunglasses, a floppy hat and hiding in a bus shelter like a character in a very poor play.

She flipped down the little plastic seat and checked it for chewing gum or other detritus – these were her best trousers after all. From her perch she could observe the front path and the porch of the shared house, so if Judy were to arrive, she shouldn't miss her. She actually crossed her fingers. How long would it be reasonable to wait? This could turn out to be a total waste of time of course. Judy didn't live here, and even if she had she was a young student, just how much time did they spend indoors in the summer anyway? But there was no other way to find her.

It would be so much easier to give up and go home.

The thought depressed her. If she were to leave and make her way back what would she be going back to exactly? Her mobile was switched off to avoid his calls, her door locked and bolted, and any knock would send her into a panic. What was she to do on this bright summer evening? Sit indoors and nurse her wounds and wait for the bruising to fade? She had never before realised the impact one moment of brutality could have on a life. Sympathy for the bruised and beaten women who found themselves at the surgery was natural, but when they walked through the exit and back into their own lives how much thought had she ever given them? None. Though she knew it was a bad idea to become involved with the lives of patients, she felt sorry now that she hadn't.

Perhaps when this was all over she could put this new and dreadful knowledge to some use. There were shelters for women in crisis, and perhaps with her experience at work and her now personal understanding of some of the issues, she could volunteer to help. It would be an honest use of her spare time and yes, she didn't think it was unrealistic to think that at least some good could come from this disaster.

She was so lost in her musings and plans that she almost missed the young woman strolling down the road opposite. In the nick of time she spotted Judy. She was alone and carrying a couple of bulging bags from the local supermarket. Mary jumped to her feet and ran across the road, terribly aware of the genuine risk that Jacob could walk around the corner at any moment and she simply did not know what she would do in that case.

"Judy, wait. Hang on a second. I need to talk to you, Judy."

The girl glanced across the road, a flash of puzzlement on her face was replaced in short order by a moment of recognition and then, as Mary whipped the hat from her head, a look of unrestrained horror.

"Shit Mary, what happened to you?" Standing now close beside the other woman Mary didn't know how to word the answer and so she said nothing, she waited a few moments before Judy's hand encumbered by the heavy bag raised to her mouth. "Jacob?" It was little above a whisper.

Mary nodded, tears had flooded her eyes and she searched in her pocket for a tissue.

"I need to speak to you, Judy. Can you come? My car is around the corner. I need help."

"Oh God, Mary. I, well I don't know, erm." She held up the bags that she was carrying; her eyes were fixed on Mary's poor face. "Look I need to drop the shopping off. Can you give me a minute? Where are you parked?"

"Just round the corner, the red Fiesta. It's just by the house with the big blue gate."

"Yeah, yeah I know it. Look, I'll drop these bags off, say hello to everyone – otherwise they'll wonder what's going on – and then I'll come and find you. Are you alright? Have you seen a doctor? God, Mary, have you called the police? I'll come with you if that's what you want. I'll come no danger, shit I tried to warn you. I should have told you straight out, shouldn't I? I feel so bad."

"No, no for heaven's sake this isn't your fault. I haven't been to the police. I'm not going to." She held up a hand as the other woman began to interrupt. "No, I have a plan though but I need your help. Will you help me, do you think you can?"

"I will if I can, Mary, of course. What a pig he is. When did he do this?"

"Look I can't talk about it now, not in the street. Will you come home with me? I don't like being out right now, looking like this, you know. Will you come back and let me tell you what I think I'd like to do?"

"Give me five minutes and then I'll come and find you."

She flopped back into the car and heaved a great sigh of relief. She had done it. She had taken the first step. Her heart was lighter and her spirits soared. She was doing something and it seemed she now had an ally.

Chapter 44

As soon as the slight figure in the denim shorts and pink T shirt came around the corner Mary started the engine. She was desperate to take herself away from this place where at any moment Jacob could appear. Her heart was thundering and her hands slick with nervous sweat. Judy gave her a little wave and trotted up to the passenger door. She slid into the car and they were driving off before she had even had the time to fasten her belt and tuck her shoulder bag into the foot well.

"Thanks, Judy, thanks so much." Mary turned and smiled at the young woman who was peering at her bruised and battered face.

"That looks really sore, and your poor eye is all swollen. Did he really do that? What did he do? Oh, look if you don't want to talk about it, I understand but – well I've just never seen this…" She flicked a hand towards Mary "…Anything like this before."

"He hit me, it's quite simple really. No, no it's not." Mary's brow creased as she corrected the statement. "It's not simple, that's not what I mean. I mean that there is no doubt, no confusion, he raised his hand and he struck me hard and knocked me to the floor. I have a huge bruise on my side where I collided with the worktop and, well, you can see what else."

"Have you been to the doctor? Don't you think you should?"

"I can't, could you? I think I'm going to be okay. It looks worse than it is." Again she stopped and thought for a moment before altering her statement. "By that I mean that I don't think there is any permanent physical damage. Once the bruises go, I feel sure it'll be fine. On the other hand, in a way you know, it's worse than it looks, isn't it? Do you know what I mean?"

Judy nodded. She understood.

Mary laid a hand on top of the girl's where they were crossed on her lap. "Thanks, Judy, for coming with me, for believing me."

"I feel so guilty though. I should have been braver. I should have come right out and told you what he did to Chloe. That's my friend you know. When I came to your house, I should have just told you. I'm so sorry, Mary. I feel as though some of this is my fault."

"Don't be silly. You didn't make me go out with him, did you? But you did try to tell me. Oh yes, and just so that we're clear, we were lovers. I don't want you wondering and imagining. I don't know how you feel about that, but there you have it. Look, will you come back to my house and let me talk to you? Do you have time?"

"Yes, of course I will."

They settled in the tidy living room and Mary switched on the table lamp; though it was still bright outside, she had dragged the heavy drapes across the window. She was terrified that Jacob would come back and so was wrapping the house around herself, making a place of safety.

"Will you have a drink with me? A glass of wine, some beer, a cup of tea?"

"What are you having?"

"If you'll have one with me, I could really do with a drink. It's a bit early but I've had a hard day and a glass of wine right now would be lovely."

"Okay, that'd be nice, have you got white?"

"I have, just hold on there."

Once the wine had been poured and a dish of nuts sat on the table between them, Mary settled in the armchair from where she could look straight into the face of her visitor.

"Okay, Judy I need to ask you something straight out is that okay?"

"Of course."

"Your friend, Chloe was it?" Judy nodded. "Did she run away from Uni because Jacob hit her?"

The response was a firm nod of affirmation.

"Yes, he hit her and stalked her and, in the end, she couldn't take it anymore, so she went back to her mum and dad's place."

"Are you still in touch with her?" Another nod.

"And she didn't go to the police, didn't take any action?"

"No, she didn't. She was too scared of him."

"Do you know why he did it? Did she tell you?"

"She said that he just lost his temper and changed in an instant. That was one of the things that she found most frightening. One minute he was perfectly nice and then BAM, he was a monster."

"Yes, that's what happened here, it was so very sudden. Do you know what caused it?"

"Not in great detail but it was something very small. Something about a text from a friend that referred to a conversation. Oh, you know it was one of those daft girly things, just a laugh, and he took offence at it."

"And you're still in touch with her?"

"Yes, I am. We've known each other for a long time. I see her at weekends if I go home, and we email each other all the time."

"Do you think she'll talk to me?"

"I don't know. I can ask her but I think she really just wants to put it behind her, you know."

"Yes, but she hasn't, has she? She has changed her whole life because of it and how do you think that will make her feel when she looks back? Don't get me wrong I do understand."

As she said this Mary unconsciously raised a hand to her damaged face.

"You see I can't go home. This is my home, and I can't just leave it and go away but what I also can't do, is live in fear. He's already caused me to change the locks and turn off my phone. I can't go on from day to day feeling afraid, wondering if I'm going to meet him on the street, or if he's going to turn up here or at the surgery. You do see, don't you?"

"Yes, I do."

"So, the only answer is for me to drive him away. I have an idea how I might be able to do that. Will you help me?"

"I will. I'll get in touch with Chloe and see if we can meet up."

Mary gave a great sigh and raised her glass in a silent salute.

Chapter 45

It was difficult to settle. Once Judy had left with a promise to phone as soon as she had spoken to Chloe, Mary made a sandwich and poured a second glass of wine. Her nerves were in turmoil. She gave herself a mental kick after Judy had gone. One thing she did need was her opinion about whether or not it would be possible to access the college social network pages in the way she wanted. The whole thing actually hinged on whether or not this girl, who she had only spoken to a couple of times, would be willing to take a huge risk on her behalf.

For the plan to work she would need access to Jacob's computer and possibly the memory card from his camera. The only way that she would be able to achieve that would be with help from Judy who could visit the shared house. Fear had stilled her tongue though in case the answer had been no and had dashed all her hopes before anything had even begun. If they arranged a meeting, all of them together, she might be able to use the emotion that would be stirred up to drive things along. It was a cynical manipulation and she felt a pang of guilt, but anyway if they decided this plan was fated from the start, as was very possible given the number of things that would need to come together, then perhaps the three of them would be able to come up with something else.

The idea that she could meet another of Jacob's victims was strangely comforting. Judy had been lovely, though she had returned over and over to the idea that she was in part responsible, and Mary hoped that if she did indeed help to drive Jacob away then she would let that unnecessary feeling of guilt go.

She turned on the television but switched it off again after a few minutes. There was nothing on it to hold her attention. She flipped through a couple of magazines without seeing anything except the blur of shiny, coloured pages. For a while she paced back and forth in the lounge, a cup of tea didn't hit the spot and she missed her friend Jane badly. In this situation it would have been perfect to have her there and to have her support. It was impossible though, on the one hand it would be simply too embarrassing to admit that Jane had been correct in her assessment all along, though the bitterness of her attack still brought a lump to Mary's throat. Aside from that was the knowledge she had phoned Mary's mum and involved her in things that were, in truth, not really her concern. If she hadn't done that then the fateful phone call would never have happened. What then? How long would it have continued and at what stage would she have discovered the truth about this man who she had truly thought she could love?

Maybe he would never have hit her. Perhaps if their relationship had developed and deepened none of this would have happened. Maybe all he needed was genuine affection and that would help him to overcome the demon that made him lash out in this dreadful way. Something must have happened to him in the past. Perhaps with the right handling, he could overcome it. He had looked so very sad standing on the step with the huge bunch of roses, desperation in his eyes. She imagined the feel of his hands on her body and the whisper of his loving words in her ears. Perhaps she was going at this all the wrong way. Of course, she could never have a love affair with him now, that thought was ridiculous, but maybe she could help him. Rather than drive him away perhaps she should be reaching out and offering kindness? She stood and as she did so the mirror caught the reflection of her ruined face. The soreness had reduced now until she hardly felt it but seeing it again, the darkening bruises and the horrible blood-shot eye, she gasped. No, nobody could be allowed to do this to another person and be offered sympathy. If he cared he would search out help himself, it wasn't her job.

As she turned back to the stairs with her resolve to act newly-strengthened, she heard tapping on the front door. Surely the bell was still working. She froze, her head tipped to one side listening. The faint, rapid knocking continued and then the cover on the letter box moved.

"Hello, Mary. Mary will you not let me in? Come on, Lovely lady. Come on you know I didn't mean to hurt you. You must know that. Come on now, let me in I want to apologise and then we can make up and be friends."

She stared in horror as his fingers crawled and reached through the tiny space and his voice, whispering in the growing darkness, filled her ears.

"Oh come on now, Mary, let me in. Won't you just let me in and we can kiss and make up?"

Chapter 46

If he lowered his eyes to the letter box Jacob would be able to see her where she sat, tense and silent on the lower steps. Should she drop to her knees and crawl to the safety of the living room or make a bid for the upstairs? His long fingers had pulled back from the narrow strip and a pink envelope had been pushed through to flop with a quiet wheeze onto the carpet. It was obviously some sort of card. There was no way she would either want to retrieve the thing or be brave enough to venture so close to where she knew he stood, even though he was safely excluded by the solid wooden door and the newly fitted locks.

Crablike, she made her way up the stairs until, upon reaching the half landing, she stood and ran the last few yards. She went to her own bedroom; the light was out and the curtains hadn't yet been drawn across the windows. By the light of the streetlamp she could peer out and see the top of his head as he shuffled back and forth on the front step.

Frustration was apparent from the way he paced in the small space, spinning to look out at the street and then back to tap yet again on the door. She wondered why he didn't use the bell but thanked her lucky stars he hadn't, for this small noise was so much easier to cope with than the intrusive ringing would be. As she watched from the darkness he glanced upward and with a gasp she jumped away from her vantage point. Her breath stilled as she waited to find whether or not he had seen her or discerned the slight movement of the curtains.

Again, he called out to her, "Mary, Mary can you hear me? The bell doesn't work."

Of course. She now realised that the locksmith must have disconnected it and with the mad flurry of action when they had locked Jacob out, they hadn't thought to check and make sure that everything was back to working order. She would have to get him back to reconnect it. He was coming anyway to check all was well and she had a bottle of whisky waiting as a thank you for his help. If only he was here now, a bulwark against this latest assault.

"Mary, for heaven's sake this is silly now. I'm sorry right, I lost my temper. Look, I admit it and I want to show you just how sorry I am."

He was keeping his voice low, no doubt aware that the neighbours would be tempted to interfere if they thought Mary was in trouble but the low hiss of his words through the evening hush was chilling. As she stood in the middle of her room, hands clasped in front of her mouth, she was as frightened as she could ever remember being in the whole of her life.

A sudden loud thud reverberated through the space between them. She gasped. His mood had changed.

"Right, you are being stupid now, aren't you? Really, there is no need for any of this. You can't stay in there forever you know. I see you changed the locks, well that was unnecessary to start with and what, you think I'll just go away now? Don't be ridiculous, we've got a thing going on here, a good thing. I'm not going to give up on you. I'll come back tomorrow. We can have a cup of coffee and a chat and you'll see how silly you are being."

She raised herself on tiptoe to allow a glimpse of the drive as he strode through the gateway and, leaving the metal gate swinging behind him, he thundered away down the road.

She flopped onto the bed and let the tears of relief and tension flood her cheeks. She drew in a deep breath and desperately tried to hold herself together.

Perhaps it was time to call the police. The jumbled thoughts fighting for supremacy in her fear-numbed mind swirled back time and again now to this. Was it time to bring in an outside authority? What would they do? They would no doubt interview her at length and in great detail. They would lay bare the things that she was embarrassed about and they would probably want to know why she had waited two days before contacting them. They would interview him of course and, though the evidence of brutality was all too obvious, then what could they do?

If it were possible she could go the whole way, take him to court, stand in the witness box and reveal, for the benefit of strangers, private and deeply personal issues. Then what? The chances that he would be incarcerated were slim, so very slim. He would possibly be given some sort of "punishment" – litter picking on the streets or cleaning up graffiti. The judge would no doubt insist that he attend an anger management course and he would be told to keep away from her. What of her? She would then spend a miserable time knowing that he may be just around the next corner, in the supermarket innocently shopping, or on the bus as he had been the first time that they had met. It wasn't any sort of future that she could contemplate and so, for better or worse, she would stick to her plan and if it failed then so be it.

Chapter 47

During the long night, tossing and turning under the covers, Mary by turn replayed all the events of the last few dreadful days and tried to clearly formulate the ideas she had. Hopefully Judy would call soon with arrangements to meet Chloe, phase one accomplished and safely tucked away.

She dragged herself from bed in the early hours and booted up the computer. Once on the college website she clicked around following links and perusing the pages of information. As she worked a conviction that they could make this happen soothed her battered nerves. The only sound was the keyboard and mouse as she made notes and bookmarked pages and by the time the birds greeted the daylight she was smiling, genuinely hopeful for the first time. She was an intelligent, strong woman and would damned well succeed in ridding her life of this blight.

The pink envelope sat beside the front door and on her way through to the kitchen Mary scooped it up. With not a moment of hesitation and not even looking at the writing on the front she stamped on the lever of the pedal bin and with a flourish she threw the thing away. She felt strong and decisive; this was the new start. A cup of strong coffee and a piece of toast further brightened the morning and she stepped out into the back garden. Ignoring the light dampness of the dew she sat at the little metal table and allowed herself to look forward to a time when her life would be pleasant and peaceful again. It would come, it had to.

The phone rang and the answering machine served up its recorded message. Although Jacob had made no attempt to use the landline, she couldn't be absolutely sure that he didn't have the number and didn't want to hear his voice, whispering down the line, pleading and cajoling. As Judy began to speak, she snatched up the handset.

"Judy, hi it's me."

"Oh, right. How are you today, how's your poor face?"

"It's okay thanks. He came back last night, Judy. I was scared stupid. He was knocking on the door and whispering through the letter box. It was absolutely horrible."

"Oh God, you poor thing. Did you call the police?"

"No. I thought about it but, no."

"Okay, it's your decision after all. Anyway listen, I've managed to contact Chloe. I've given her an idea of what's happened and told her you would like to meet her. I have to tell you, she isn't keen. She just wants to put it all behind her and hasn't even told her mum and dad the real reason for dropping out. They think she just wanted to be nearer home. She said it was terrible how it made her look like a wimp but by then she just needed to feel safe. Anyway, I managed to talk her round. She did have some erm – well I suppose you would call them conditions. She wants to meet you somewhere away from her home, not here though, she was adamant about that. There's no way she's coming anywhere near where he is. I suppose you can understand that eh?"

"Yes, I know just how she feels believe me. What else was there?"

"She said that even though she'll meet you that's as far as it goes for now, she's given up such a lot because of him and is not prepared to let him take anything else."

Mary sighed. "I do understand. I hope she'll feel able to do what I'm asking, but if she's not that's fine. I'll carry on by myself. It won't work as well but I'll still do it. Anyway, look did you arrange for us to see her?"

"I did, can you manage today?"

"Oh yes, brilliant, of course. Where?"

"There's a pub near where she's living now and we can go there and have some lunch. There's just one thing though."

"Yeah, go on."

"Can you drive? It's a fair way. It'll use quite bit of petrol. I can only afford two trips in any one month and I want to go home next week for my mum's birthday."

"Oh, of course I wouldn't have it any other way. I'll treat us all to lunch as well. You've been great, Judy. You really have. I'll see you in a little while then."

"Yes, I'll come to your house about eleven if that's okay? And that'll give us plenty of time to get up there."

"Great, I'll see you soon. Thanks, oh thanks so much."

It was exciting and hopeful but now it was down to her to convince these two young women that the plan was viable and also to make them want to help her. She changed into jeans and a soft top and fished out her sunglasses but didn't put on any make up. The bruising was so much more obvious without it and it was essential for her now to win their sympathy.

Chapter 48

She was tiny, and very pretty. A small dark-haired girl with brown eyes and a shy smile. Chloe was already waiting for them when Judy and Mary arrived at the pub. It was a generic sort of place, old books lined the window ledges, and there were a couple of glass fronted cupboards stacked with miscellaneous pieces of china. But they weren't there for the ambience.

"I'll get us all a drink," Mary said, her purse already in her hand. These were students and undoubtedly counting their cash and she was determined they wouldn't be inconvenienced by helping her. "What would you like?"

"I'll have a glass of lager thanks." Judy had slipped into the seat next to the window and the two girls embraced, obviously close friends.

"What would you like Chloe? I think I'll have wine but just a small one. If we're eating it should be okay, I think. Are you driving?"

"No, I came on the train, the station is just up the road there and it's not far. I'd love a glass of wine actually."

"Right, and have you got a menu?"

The preliminaries taken care of, there was an awkward moment as everyone waited for someone else to make the first move. Mary decided that it must be up to her as she was the one who had orchestrated the meeting and indeed the one who was looking for favours.

"Thanks so much for meeting us Chloe. I hope you are okay with this."

The other girl took a breath and glanced around.

"I have to say I was a bit cross at first – with Judy."

As she said this, she reached across the table to lay her hand over that of the other young woman.

"It's okay, I'm not mad anymore but I was. I had put it all behind me you see. I had given up a life I was enjoying, and it took me ages to find another course here and well, living at home is fine, its good but it's not what I thought would be happening to me right now. I hated the fact that I'd been forced to run back home, and I hated him for making that happen, but I had moved on. When you rang, Judy, I was cross and upset but then – well I thought about what you said – that he had gone back to the college and was still doing what he did to me." Here she raised her hand, indicating Mary's bruised face. "Now I see what's happened to you, I'm glad I said yes actually."

"What do you mean gone back?" Mary was puzzled by the statement.

"Well he left as well. About the same time as I came back home he took a year out and went back to where he came from. He told the others at his digs that he was going to travel but another mate of ours, you remember Charlie, don't you Judy?" Judy gave a short nod. "I'm still in touch with him, and he said he went back home and didn't do anything for the whole year. He didn't even get a job. He lived in a flat with his brother and that was all. I don't know much more than that. There was talk that he was stressed but it was very vague."

"So, he didn't go home to his mum and dad?" Judy asked. This was obviously news to her. While they talked Mary just kept silent, absorbing the information.

"No, he doesn't get on with his parents. I don't know all the details but it's to do with his sister, the clever one. But he wouldn't talk about it when we were together and that was the cause of the first big row to be honest."

Now she paused and took a long drink.

"I wasn't being nosey you know, just interested. We'd been together for a while and I just asked him if he was going to introduce me to his parents. I didn't think that I was being pushy but when he just said no I suppose I did bring it up a couple more times, and then one day he just snapped. One minute he seemed okay and the next, well, I think you can guess, eh Mary. I don't think his dad is around anymore, to be honest they're not the lovely close family he had me believe."

"So, that's why he was registering with the doctor and so on. I did wonder how come he was doing that if he'd been there long enough to have had a relationship with you."

"Yes, they let him just take a gap."

"But, correct me here if I've got the wrong end of the stick but Judy said she thought it was about a phone call and you talking to a friend, the time he was violent."

Chloe lowered her gaze and fiddled with the glass tipping it this way and that. When she looked up there were tears quivering on the ends of her long lashes. "That was the second time."

Mary gasped. "Oh God, you mean…"

"Yes, I know, I do know. I was stupid but I thought I loved him and he was so sorry and he cried, he did, he cried and he was so lovely and I believed him. He said he would get help, anger management, and he needed me to help him. I suppose I was vain. I suppose I thought I could help him, my ego you know."

"No, no that's one thing I do know, you mustn't blame yourself for any of it. Nothing excuses him raising his hand to you, nothing. No matter what mistakes you made, whatever you did or didn't do, he is the one at fault. You must know that."

"Well, I do now. I did the second time, after I came back home, gave up everything I'd worked so hard for and scuttled back here to lick my wounds, huh literally. Then I saw what an idiot I'd been. I did wonder. It's probably silly but I did wonder if he was running away. He knew I'd decided to leave and perhaps he thought I was going to cause trouble and so he, you know, got in first, but it's probably not like that. Do you think? They wouldn't cover up for him would they, the college?

"Anyway, there we are. So, what is it you want from me Mary? Judy said she didn't know what the plan was but you wanted to try and drive him away. I don't know how you can do that, even the police wouldn't be able to do that I don't think."

"Well if my plan works there won't be any option left to him but to leave. That's what I want. I need to make sure that there is nothing left for him to stay for and no real option for him to come back."

At that point the meals arrived and, as the fuss with cutlery and sauces filled the space, Mary collected her thoughts ready to put forward her case.

Chapter 49

Mary took a deep breath, laid down her knife and fork and took a sip of her wine.

"I might as well get down to it I suppose."

She smiled at the other two women at the table who turned and waited silently. She did notice that Chloe had taken hold of Judy's hand, the gesture and all that lay behind it touched her heart.

"Chloe, I want you to know before I start that if you tell me to get lost, I do fully understand, and I won't think any the worse of you. I know what I am going to ask is hard, okay."

Chloe bit her lip and nodded.

"A great deal of what I'm hoping to do hinges on the answer to a rather strange question and I have a horrible feeling that it's going to be the first stumbling block but here we go. When I was beaten by Jacob, I took a photograph of my face. I took several actually and made copies. I wasn't really sure why at the time but now I'm glad I did because it is the kingpin of my plan. I don't suppose you did that did you, Chloe? Did you by any chance take any pictures or were any taken in the days immediately afterwards. Anything that shows what he did?"

Mary's fingers were tightly crossed under the table and she hardly dared to breathe as she waited for the answer. What were the chances really. How many women would choose to take a photograph of themselves bruised and battered?

For a moment no one spoke. Chloe lowered her eyes.

"I did, after the second time."

She nibbled at her lower lip, a habit that Mary had already observed, a little sign that she was struggling to hold it all together. They waited for her to go on.

"When it happened the second time, it was so awful. I had been talking to my friend Zoe on the phone and we'd been giggling about a television programme we'd seen. Jacob had come in half-way through and somehow formed the impression we were talking about our boyfriends."

Here she looked to Judy.

"You remember Zoe? She was going out with that nice guy Matt then. I think they are living together now."

Judy nodded and smiled encouragingly at her friend.

"Well, Jake sat on the settee for a bit and I didn't even notice he was listening until we finished the call and then…"

She took another gulp of air and blew out her cheeks. Mary wanted to tell her to stop and say it didn't matter, she didn't need to put herself through it, but that wasn't true.

"Anyway, I finished my call, I turned to him and was about to tell him what Zoe had been saying and, well I didn't have the chance. He grabbed me by the arm and dragged me across the room. He was yelling at me the whole time, 'Gossip, gossip. Bloody little chatterers, having a laugh at me, were you? All having a good old giggle?' I was gobsmacked. We hadn't been doing that at all for one thing, but even if we had, well his reaction was so over the top. I struggled and tried to get free but he had tight hold of me and then he started to hit me. He hit me across the face a couple of times actually and I fell but he was still holding my arm and it twisted, God that hurt. Then he dragged me up again and sort of threw me away from him. I collided with the table and that was what broke my tooth I think."

"You broke your tooth? Oh Chloe."

Mary had leaned across the table to take hold of the girl's hand. Tears streamed down her face.

"Yes, and I had a black eye. He grabbed me by the hair then and dragged me up and flung me onto the settee. 'That'll teach you to gossip about me.' He was yelling and I was crying and it was just awful. Then he just stormed out.

"I locked the door after him, and it was the last time I spoke to him. The next morning, I went to the dentist. I told him a door had hit me in the face. I don't know whether he believed me but anyway it didn't matter. He couldn't do much just then because of all the swelling and so I packed up and ran back home to my mum and dad. I told them I'd had an accident in a friend's car, I lied to them and I hated doing it but I couldn't tell them the truth. I was too ashamed. Anyway, I got my tooth fixed, and Judy packed up my stuff for me, for which I'm eternally grateful."

She leaned across and kissed the other girl.

"The point is yes, I took pictures. I took them so that if he ever came back, if he ever got in touch or tried to reach me I would have them and I would look at them and I would never, ever let anyone do something like that to me ever again."

As they looked at each other over the detritus of the pub meal they cobbled together watery smiles, joined hands and Mary knew that she was over one of the biggest hurdles. She had allies and more, she had friends to help her.

Chapter 50

They sat in the pub for several hours. Mary bought them more drinks and then coffee.

There were times when she thought she had lost them. Though Judy agreed what she was proposing was possible, she hesitated when asked if stealing the information from Jacob's computer and camera was beyond what was reasonable. They were all decent people, and to interfere in someone's life to the extent they were planning and to impact in such a negative way on Jacob's future was a step into the darkness for them.

Mary almost threw in her hand at one point. Judy had agreed to go along with the plan if Chloe would play her part but when Mary asked the girl to let her have images of her battered face for publishing on the internet, she shook her head decisively.

"No way. I couldn't, I just couldn't. It was horrendous. I know your poor face is badly damaged Mary but mine was so much worse and then there was my tooth. Well, it was so bad that my mum and dad believed me with no hesitation when I told them I'd been in a car crash. I can't let that go out there, sorry but no."

"If we make sure you can't be recognised?"

"Ha, that's a laugh, no way would anyone recognise me from that. It's not that, it's just, you know it would be there and I would be scared of just coming across it you know. I'm still in touch with some of my friends from those days, and what you are proposing would have them all in a dither and sharing and tweeting and it would be me, about me, do you see? I'm sorry but I can't."

Her dark hair swung around her face as she shook her head back and forth in distress.

"Okay, I do understand and I told you right from the start I wouldn't ask you to do anything that was too much, so fair enough. I am still going ahead though and if you see this stuff and your friends are tweeting about it and discussing it on Facebook would you promise me you would let them know you saw me in real life and you know what I am saying is true? Could you at least do that?"

Chloe nodded her head and then lowered her face into her hands.

"God, Mary you make me feel such a wuss, you really do. You are being so brave about this."

"I have to, Chloe. I have no choice. You were able to come back here and pick up your life again. I know it wasn't the life you had chosen but I think it's worked out for you anyway hasn't it? I haven't got that option, you see. My home is all I have. My home and my family are my world and I can't up and leave and start again somewhere else. I know all I can do is try to make my place safe and peaceful again and so, yes, I suppose that is making me determined."

There was a pause, the old clock in the corner of the room ticked. Around them the mutter of conversation and the clink of glasses filled the brittle moments as Chloe battled with inner demons that were not of her own making. Eventually she raised her eyes.

"Okay, look I'll tell you what. If you promise never to give my name to anyone, even if they try to guess — and let's face it anyone who knew me could put two and two together – if you promise you will never confirm it, and I approve the picture before it goes out, then okay, I'll go along with you."

"Oh, Chloe thank you. That is amazing."

Mary leaped to her feet and leaned across the table to embrace the other girl awkwardly amidst the coffee cups and glasses.

The sun was lowering by the time they left with warm hugs and promises to keep in touch. The darkening sky was streaked with rose. Blackbirds filled the evening with liquid music and Mary drank in the beauty. She held it close and told herself it was a blessing on her plans, a sign of success, and of a gentle future back in control of her own destiny.

The drive home was pleasant and uneventful and she dropped Chloe at her digs with an arrangement to meet the next day and set the thing in motion. As she waved to her new friend and turned for home there was no forewarning of what was waiting at the end of the long day.

Chapter 51

As soon as the door closed, she knew. At first glance the house appeared the same as it had been when she left, but the atmosphere was different. There were no tell-tale noises, no smell. It was – a feeling. Her heart thudding Mary stepped slowly along the hallway. The atmosphere was thick with threat. Someone had been in while she was away. Her brain was quickly sifting information. The locks had been changed, the new keys were all safely in her purse, and she hadn't even had the chance to leave a spare with her mother, which was the usual procedure.

The light in the hall was different. The kitchen door was closed. She never closed the door to her kitchen and the borrowed light was usually enough to brighten the narrow space.

She stopped. Her instincts were to run, turn and get out of the place, get into the car and leave. She pushed the feelings back. Where was there to run to and from what? The past few days had disrupted all her senses, maybe this was just part of her confusion. Perhaps she had inadvertently closed the door. Why, after years of living in the place, would she suddenly do that? But, maybe. She took a few more steps, her hands shook, fear stalked alongside her on the carpet.

She reached and grasped the handle. It felt strange, unusual to be opening this door. She pushed at the wood. The small draught stroked at her face and made her hair wisp and move in the disturbance of air. The light was on. Soft music played from the sound system, only now with the door open could she hear it.

A vase of lilies was centrally placed on the table.

Her knees wobbled as a gasp escaped her throat. She clutched at the door frame to hold herself upright. A couple more steps took her fully into the room. The outside door was closed but the curtain on the window shifted and billowed slightly. It was an old sash-style window open just a few inches, enough to disturb the atmosphere, enough to tell her that someone had been here. He must have come through the window and then almost closed it behind him.

Her heart juddered and nausea threatened. At what point would he leap from his hiding place? Just when would he confront her and then what? She should run, while there was still time, run, run. She turned and flung back the lounge door expecting him to be there, waiting, just waiting but the room was empty and undisturbed.

She heaved a great sigh, now what should she do? As time slid by, calm was winning the battle over panic. The flowers were evidence that he had been there but perhaps that was all it was, although it was a strange and terrifying gesture to be sure.

The stairs stretched above her, the dimness of the landing taunting her until she flicked the light switch. Squaring her shoulders, she gripped the banister and planted her feet firmly on the first step, the second, third, onward and upward.

The bathroom called her, fear had weakened her bladder, so she ran in and relieved herself. As she sat on the little wooden seat, she let go the tears of tension and terror and lowered her head into her hands allowing the sobbing to engulf her for a few moments. She gathered herself together, blew her nose on a piece of toilet paper and then dragged off her jacket. She rinsed her hands and strode along the landing to her bedroom.

Her room was dimly lit by golden light. Candles burned on the dresser and the bedside table. They were newly lit. The tiny flames guttered and flickered in the breeze from the half-opened window. The bed, carefully made as always was strewn with red rose petals and on the chest an ice bucket held a bottle with the top loosened and the cork pushed partway in. A solitary champagne flute stood beside it with a tiny card propped against the stem.

The picture of a smiling teddy holding a bunch of daisies mocked her, and Jacob had scrawled inside with a red pen.

> *Enjoy this on your own, lovely lady, but maybe we can share the next one. I miss you. X*

The room spun as reality floated away. Mary felt herself succumbing to the horror and flopped onto the side of the bed and lowered her head to her knees. As her senses returned, she became aware of the rattle and click of the gate as he left.

Chapter 52

She tore at the bedding. Scarlet petals flew around her legs and fluttered dejectedly to the floor. Everything was ripped from the bed; pillows, duvet, sheets and all were bundled onto the landing. She had extinguished the candles and now, as the wax cooled and hardened, she gathered them together and dumped them into the bin. Next, she turned to the sparkling wine in its bucket of rapidly melting ice. Grabbing it by the neck she headed for the door on her way to the kitchen bin. As the cold glass and a trickle of moisture cooled her hands, she looked at the green bottle. She dragged out the cork and for the first time in her life took a great slug from the neck of the bottle.

It was good.

She took another.

The alcohol hit her immediately and a giggle burbled up from deep in her gut as she caught a glimpse of herself in the bedroom mirror; clothes dishevelled, hair wild, clutching a bottle of what was in reality cheap plonk. She began to laugh, veering towards the edge of hysteria. She flopped onto the floor, her back resting against the bedroom wall and raised the bottle again to her lips.

What the hell was she going to do?

There was the plan, and with Judy to help her, she still hoped that it would be enough to make life for Jacob untenable at the college. She had to believe this plan would work otherwise any future for her was hopeless. The thought of leaving her home and moving away was painful and, if he didn't clear off, there wasn't going to be another option.

Should she call the police? Her home had been invaded and her safety threatened. She squeezed her eyes closed and spoke into the darkness.

"Oh Mary, what the heck are you doing?"

There was of course no answer and she was swept by a wave of loneliness and isolation.

The bottle was now a third empty and with a shrug she filled the glass which still sat on the table. Perched on the bedroom chair she laid back her head and sipped at the cool liquid. The wine had worked its magic to an extent and her heart felt lighter, though she knew it was an illusion and the influence of alcohol was no answer at all. She stood and began to tidy up the mess. She remade her bed with clean linen, all of it. She couldn't tell if he'd lain across her covers, or whether his traitorous fingers had caressed and held her pillows, her nightwear. It all had to go, there must be no trace of him.

When everything was clean and tidy she made her way back to the kitchen. It was sad to discard the blameless blooms but the flowers had to go, and she tore the little card into tiny pieces and tossed it in the bin. Sensible Mary knew that she should make tea, but the Mary of this night, with her tumultuous emotions and shredded nerves, needed oblivion and she poured more of the wine and glugged it back.

"Sufficient unto the day is the evil thereof," she muttered quietly and then, "All things must pass."

It was the wine talking she knew, but the aphorisms helped, though in real terms they were empty words against a full-on threat.

As she slipped between the clean bedcovers and lowered her reeling head onto the pillow, the tears began and she let them flow. They followed so many others she had shed recently and in a slew of self-pity she railed at the fates who had first taken her husband and then offered her excitement and the chance of love, only to dash it all against the rocks of a reality that she never would have believed she would face.

Tomorrow Judy was coming and they could get started on the plan but for tonight she simply gave herself up to misery and ignored the feelings of guilt that such weakness inevitably threw in her path.

Chapter 53

Her head pounded, her mouth felt as if she had licked out the wheelie bin and when she tried to open her eyes the happy morning light screamed onto her retinas like lashings of molten mercury. It was years and years since Mary had suffered from a hangover and now, gulping back the nausea and trying to drag herself from bed, she was reminded in full measure of nights at Uni. And mornings in bed sits with groaning friends and deep regrets.

The pounding was getting heavier and was joined by a shrill ringing in her ears. There was an urgent need to make it to the bathroom, her bladder was complaining and her stomach threatened at any moment to erupt.

"Oh God. You stupid woman." She muttered to herself in disgust.

The ringing was louder now, and she realised with a thud of horror that it was the front doorbell. Judy, Judy was coming over first thing. She pulled open the door.

"Morning, oh Mary, whatever is the matter, you look ghastly?"

"Come in, go into the kitchen. Can you put the kettle on? Look Judy, I have been really stupid but will you stay? Just make a cup of coffee or whatever, I really, really need a shower and then when I come back down, I'll tell you what has happened. It was horrible. Just horrible. Do you mind?"

"No, no it's fine. You carry on. I'll make some tea, shall I?"

"Oh yes, please."

Feeling a little better after a quick shower Mary joined Judy who was waiting at the kitchen table, sipping at a mug of tea and nibbling a piece of toast.

"Okay, truth time. I've got a thundering hangover. I am so sorry, Judy. I was really silly; I drank a whole bottle of fizzy wine and went to bed completely drunk. I can't imagine what you must think of me but I can explain."

"Hey, you don't need to explain to me. What you do is your concern. Really, don't stress."

"Well, that's lovely of you but the thing is that when I got back last night, he'd been here. Actually, there is a good chance that when I came in, that he was still here. It really freaked me out and I reacted stupidly and now I'm paying for it." She gave a rueful grin.

Judy had walked around the table and was now kneeling beside Mary where she slumped on the little dining chair.

"You poor thing. He's a real weirdo, he really is. Look, let's get this thing started. I've been planning it out. You said that you have a VPN set up here, don't you?"

Mary nodded. She had set up the Virtual Private Network a while ago when she had been worried about a chat room she had used briefly.

"Right, well we can use that and I will get everything set up now. Then I'll go to the house and see if I can get access to his stuff. I'm worried about that bit Mary. I mean I've never done anything like this before."

"I know, and it's a lot to ask, and if you don't want to do it, I understand I really do."

"No, when I look at you, your poor face and now the state that you're in today, well – he just can't do this. I'll see what I can do. If I can get access to his computer and find where his stuff is, I'll copy what I can. What we really need though is the stuff that he's got for his Degree Show. That's the work that he will have worked most on and it can't be published before the exhibition or it will be disallowed. That's the stuff we need. It's only about three weeks now until it has to be presented, so he should have it nearly ready. I asked Brian about it all. He's on the same course and so I know what I'm looking for.

"Chloe sent me copies of her pictures. I blanked out her eyes and sent copies back and she has said yes, go ahead and use them. So, when we get yours and providing I can get to Jacob's machine today, then we have all we need. The pictures of Chloe are ghastly, she was right when she said nobody would recognise her, but I did a bit of Photoshop on her eyes and hair and so on just to be sure. I also made a statement saying that we had done that. We don't want anyone coming back later saying the stuff has been doctored, so I thought it best to be up front about it. Is that all okay?"

"Oh Judy, it's more than okay, it's fantastic. How can I thank you?"

"Oh, come on. We can't let him get away with this. I mean, who could be next eh? We have to stop him."

"You show me where your PC is, get it all booted up and then while you get dressed, I'll get started. Do you want another cup of tea?"

"Oh yes please." And so it began.

Chapter 54

While Judy's fingers dabbed and flexed over the keys, Mary sat on the settee nursing a cup of tea, a thumping head and a churning stomach. Although it was great to have the plan on its way, she felt absolutely dreadful. It seemed such a short time since her world had been calm and, though it was relatively unexciting, she had been in control and there had been many pleasant days. Her job was fulfilling, this little home was a haven, her friends and family were precious and now it had all crumbled.

Half asleep in the warm room she relived that first day when the fall at the bus stop had brought all of this into her life and she marvelled at the fickleness of fate. Closing her eyes, she allowed the thoughts and remembrances to drift. He had been so lovely, such a considerate and careful lover. As the memory flipped through her mind, she felt a tiny quiver of warmth deep inside. How could it be, this beautiful, gentle young man had thrown her into such turmoil and fear?

Greyness filled her lids, tiny flashes of muted colour drifted in the void and she felt her body becoming heavy. She allowed herself to go with the peace and when Bill came and stood before her, she wasn't surprised. He was tall and strong, unmarked by the long illness and his eyes shone with love. He reached for her and with no hesitation she leaned to him.

"Mary, hey Mary, sorry but I need your input. Sorry to wake you."

Judy was shaking her shoulder very gently and with regret she left the warmth of Bill's love and dragged herself back to reality.

"Oh sorry, I drifted off there. I feel so bad about this I really do. I'm being no help at all. What do you need me to do?"

"I need the photographs of you, the ones of your face. I have put Chloe's up there and I have it all ready for the things I'm hoping to get from Jacob, and I need your pictures now. Then I want to show you what I've done. How are you feeling?"

"Actually, a bit better to be honest. I think I'll make something to eat. Do you want to have some soup with me and some toast?"

"Yeah, that sounds nice.

"Mary, don't let all this get you down. You look really sad now. If you don't want to carry on, we can stop."

"Oh, I want to carry on. I admit I'm feeling a bit low right now but it's my own fault isn't it? It's just the hangover, and a bit of shame. I feel very stupid."

"Hey, come on, don't beat yourself up. You've been through a lot."

Mary stood and threw her arms around the younger woman.

"You know, you really are a lovely person. If nothing else comes out of this but that I have met you, that's good."

"Oh, stop it. Come on, come and look at the programme and then I think you mentioned soup?"

Mary dragged a straight chair over to the desk and the two women sat side by side peering at the screen.

"Right, so what I've done is a little video. It starts, well it will if I get the images I want, with a picture of him. We want to make absolutely sure there is no doubt who we are talking about.

Then some of his shots, I don't know maybe about six or seven, and then this text: 'This is the work of Jacob Chadwick.' Then some more images. These will flip up automatically and then the text again: 'This is the work of Jacob Chadwick.' I'm hoping that by then people will be hooked and when we have them POW. The pictures of you and Chloe, side by side with the text: 'And this is the work of Jacob Chadwick. Is this a man you want to call friend?'

"So, what do you think?"

"Absolutely brilliant. It's perfect, exactly what I had in mind."

"The images I want to get will be the ones from his final show and that will effectively knock his chances of a degree on the head. Anyway, I hope that the furore this causes will get him thrown out anyway. It was a great idea Mary. I am impressed that you came up with it, I really am.

"Now, about this soup. I have to get back to the house in an hour and I want to call at the shops so that I have a legitimate excuse for going. I do the shopping for me and Steve. If luck is with us and Jacob is at the college, I should be able to get access to his stuff. They all just leave their laptops in the living room normally so fingers crossed."

"But what about passwords and stuff like that?"

"Yeah, it could be a problem but all I can do is have a go. This is my world though Mary and it's best if I don't tell you too much about what we get up to."

Judy gave a cheeky grin and a wink as they made their way to the kitchen.

Chapter 55

"Right I think I need to be getting on. Thanks so much for lunch."

"Oh, you're welcome; it was nice to have company. To be honest I've been feeling a bit isolated. Actually, that brings me to something I was meaning to ask you, Judy."

"Yeah?"

"I had to turn off my mobile phone, he was texting. Anyway, I want to check now of course and see if there is anything on there that I need to know about. I know my mum would have used the land line but..." Mary shook her head. "Well the thing is, would you mind, if I turn it on could you just have a whizz through it and delete all the messages from him? I know I'm being a wimp but to be honest I feel so worn out with it all, after last night you know..."

"Oh yeah, sure, no probs. Give it to me."

Mary pressed the power button. It paraded through the boot sequence, beeping and chiming and the little screen brightened as if happy to be back.

Judy pursed her lips.

"Well, there're over sixty messages and from the look of it a load of them are from him. What do you want me to do, just delete them?"

"Yes please."

"Right, here we go."

With her fingers dancing on the keys Judy sat at the table wiping out the attempts at contact and muttering under her breath. "Jacob, Jacob, Jacob, another, another." And so it went on for a couple of minutes.

"Oh, oh here's one from somebody called Jane. What do you want me to do, shall I just leave it or...?"

Mary held out her hand, what was this now? More upset and disturbance? She had pushed the memory of the restaurant lunch to the back of her mind and now in light of all that had happened it was even more painful. It wasn't that Jane had been correct in her assessment of the situation, indeed the things that had happened hadn't even been on her radar. She had been scathing about Jacob taking advantage, of not caring about her but simply wanting a meal ticket and in the event that had been very far from the truth. In his own warped and twisted way he cared too much. However, in her mind that day had very much been the start of the whole thing collapsing.

Mary, I miss you. I'm sorry, can we talk? – Jane

It wasn't what she had been expecting and she nodded.

"Just leave it there would you, Judy? I need to think about that one." Although Jane's attitude was still appalling in Mary's eyes, perhaps now when she needed friends, she should go some way to healing the rift.

"Oh, here's another one from Jane, shall I leave it?"

"Can you read it to me?"

Mary, please just give me a call. I just want to apologise. I was out of order.

"So, is that your mate? Have you had a row?"

"Yes, we did. It was about Jacob. She thought it was disgusting, him and me. She said I was old enough to be his mother and that he was probably only after somewhere to live or even money." Mary raised a hand to the fading bruises on her cheek. "She was wrong in that wasn't she? Tell me something Judy, what did you think? You sussed out that there was something going on with us, did you think it was disgusting?"

"Shit no, that sort of thing, age and so on, it doesn't matter anymore does it? I mean half the time you can't tell how old anyone is anyway, but that's not the point is it? You find love, wherever it is, don't you? I know that there are lots and lots of cases where two people in a relationship may have a different agenda but I don't know that it really matters. If everybody is happy and nobody gets hurt, I think any friendship, any caring, is good. No, I was worried though, I knew about Chloe and I didn't know how close you and him were, and I didn't know if it was any of my concern. In the end I should have done more and I'll always feel bad about that. You know we are always so careful, aren't we? Hesitating to interfere and if I'd told you the truth up front..."

She shrugged thin shoulders and lowered her gaze back to the little phone where she continued to censor and delete messages.

"Don't feel bad, Judy. I really do understand, and you know, at the end of the day I don't know what my reaction would have been if you had told me. I was besotted, flattered and excited and I wanted to believe in it. I should have known better. People like me, ordinary people, we don't do things like that, have affairs with boys and have sex in the afternoon... Oh God, I'm sorry I shouldn't have said that – have I embarrassed you?"

She looked across the table as Judy's body began to shake, imperceptibly at first and then as the giggling grew, she put down the phone and raised hands to her face.

"Mary. You are funny. No, I'm not embarrassed but really, why shouldn't you? What did you ever do to make you undeserving? I know your hubby died but you didn't, and you weren't doing any harm. Here, that's him deleted. I'm going to go now and I'll come back later."

She put down the mobile phone and then as she pushed to her feet she spoke again.

"If you don't mind me poking my nose in, Mary, call your friend. Have a talk, make peace. You'll probably find that she meant well and only reacted the way that she did because she cares about you."

"But it was very bigoted – what she said."

Another shrug of the thin shoulders was the only response.

After closing and locking the door behind Judy, she picked up the phone and looked at the messages from Jane. She mused for a moment on the uncomplicated and tolerant wisdom of the young. Yes, she would call her, they could talk, but not yet. When it was all over and she felt safe again, it would be nice to have her old friend back and maybe there was a chance that they could retrieve something of the old closeness.

As she turned to place the little plastic gadget on the hall table it chimed and in the message window she saw his name, Jacob. She sighed and held down the power button.

Chapter 56

After another pot of coffee and a nap, Mary was feeling pretty much back to normal. She had studied the computer programme Judy was working on and in truth, yes, she did feel quite tickled that she had come up with the plan. She needed him to go away and was honest enough to admit she wanted to feel some degree of revenge. If it all worked out, his degree delayed at the least and completely unachievable at best and him gone from the area, it would suffice.

A little thrill of excitement brought a smile to her pale face. It did begin to look as though there would be an end to this awful period and then she could gather herself and move forward. She crossed her fingers and, closing her eyes, sent out a wish that Judy would be able to gain access to the images on Jacob's computer today if possible, but at any rate soon.

She tidied the house a little and began to get some food together for an evening meal, hopefully for them to share, her and her "comrade in arms". She was so very lucky to have Judy on her side. A caring and intelligent young woman, maybe this could be the start of a longer lasting friendship. That would be nice. With no children in the family there weren't many young people to mix with and the thought of a different perspective on things was appealing.

Chopping and slicing at the kitchen counter she felt as near to happy as she had for a while. The radio played softly in the background and the sounds of road and garden combined to make her feel "at home" in a way that had seemed for a while to be out of reach.

In real terms she supposed that the physical assault, though appalling, was much less than some women put up with over and over, but it had done so much more than simply hurt her body and face. Her soul felt bruised and her security and sense of place had been ripped asunder in that one moment of mindless violence. Lost as she was in the musing, the doorbell when it sounded speared into her consciousness. A lightning flash that set her heart pounding. She dropped the knife and spun to stare down the hallway towards the front door.

A glance at the clock told her what she already knew, it was still too early to expect Judy back. After four o'clock the girl had told her and it was barely three.

She needed to look out of the bay window. If she stepped out of the kitchen to make her way to the living room her shadow would pass across the translucent glass in the front door. She would need to drop to the floor and crawl on all fours down the hall carpet. Like an insect she would need to pass along the narrow space, scuttling like a creature. She pushed away from the kitchen counter and sidled sideways across the space. The bell chimed again, a double sound, whoever was there was becoming insistent. The letter box rattled. She turned and paced quickly to the back door to check that it was locked, and the window, to ensure that it was fully located and the catch was fastened.

The bell sounded again. She was beginning to wish she had left it disconnected but it had been so easy to replace the tiny plastic plug.

Her mobile phone still lay in the hall. No matter what, she was going to have to leave the kitchen. She lowered herself to the floor. Like a cowed dog she was to crawl around her house, what had he done to her?

She scrambled to the hall table and reached to retrieve the phone. She turned it on and the happy little jingle told her over and over that there were text messages just sitting waiting for her, six of them, all of them from him.

A thunderous knocking sounded on the wood of the front door. *Oh please, go away, just go away, leave me alone.*

Sticking as close as she could to the wall, she made her way to the living room and then she pushed to her feet and stepped to the window. As she did the sound of the front gate clanging shut told her that he was gone.

She pulled aside the curtain and saw, crossing the road towards her little red car, Jane. As she reached the vehicle she looked back at the house, raised her eyes to the bedroom windows and then with a shake of her head she leaned to open the car door and get inside.

A sense of relief swept through Mary's body to be followed instantly by a sense of deep sadness that she had been reduced to a terrified crawling wreck in her own home and that, in turn, engendered a deep sense of shame. How could she allow this to happen? She had thought herself sensible and well-grounded, where in truth she was as vulnerable as any battered spouse or abused girlfriend. How quickly the fear of physical harm had reduced her to this.

She went back to the kitchen and poured a glass of cold water, her hands shook and as she sank to the kitchen chair and gazed around at the peaceful little room she felt a sense of something she hadn't known existed inside her – for the first time in her life she experienced a deep sense of hate, pure and unalloyed, it swept through her system and she gasped at the strength of it.

Chapter 57

By the time Judy came back Mary had managed to calm her shredded nerves and had made a meal for them both.

"Can you stay and eat with me?"

"Yeah, yeah why not that'd be lovely. First of all, though, let me tell you what happened."

"Right."

"Okay, so it's all good. He wasn't there, Steve was, but he fell asleep – he's a proper dormouse sometimes. Anyway, I found Jake's laptop. Shit, I'll be honest I went into his room. It wasn't in the lounge. I had a hunt and I thought, oh what the heck, in for a penny in for a pound. It was on his desk. He hasn't even got any decent password protection. It was easy peasy. Course I was rushing a bit and so I didn't sort through or anything but I just copied everything I could from his images file. I hope there's something there that we can use."

"Judy, I need to make absolutely sure that you're okay with all of this. I would hate for you to suffer because of what you've done. Before it's too late, think very carefully about what we are about to do. This is pretty much the last chance for you to back out and I wouldn't blame you if you did."

"No, no I've already thought about it. First of all, I don't think that they will link me to it anyway. We're using your VPN and I hardly know Jacob and we aren't on the same course or anything. The thing is though, even if I was worried about the repercussions, I would still want to do it. I hate what he did. To be honest when he came back after his year out, I was horrified, and I didn't know what I could do about it. Then when I saw you guys together, I had to try and warn you but this," she said holding up the little blue memory stick, "this is justice. I think so. If the plan works and we mess up the rest of his career plans and his reputation and segregate him from his friends, well yeah it's a sort of justice."

"I'll pour us a drink and then we can have a look at the stuff on the stick."

They plugged in the device and Judy's fingers flew across the keyboard. Lists and menus popped onto the screen to be superseded by others, images flicked on and off and Mary held her breath. Suddenly Judy punched the air in excitement.

"Yes, yes, there it is look. That folder – it's labelled Degree Show – well obviously that's it. Brilliant." She opened the folder and began to sort through the images and videos. The work was impressive, there were some beautiful shots of the buildings in the town and others taken of locations further afield. It was of a professional standard and in spite of herself Mary was impressed.

There was a separate subfolder with Videos, and they opened them one at a time. They had no labels but simply reference numbers. Boats, birds, some mock fashion shoots, a short playlet; all well shot, some in the middle of editing and some which looked finished.

They were about half-way through when Judy clicked on a folder labelled M1. It was a video shot in a dim room with only breathing on the soundtrack. Something tickled at the back of Mary's mind as she watched it. A sixth sense made the hairs on her arms prickle and before she realised what she was looking at her body had stilled, and her nerves were on alert.

"Stop it a second, Judy. Can you just sort of freeze it? Can you make it brighter?"

"Yeah, I think so. Hang on."

A slider bar appeared, and Judy grabbed the arrow with the mouse pointer and brightened the scene. As she did both women gasped and Mary's hand flew to her mouth.

"Stop, oh Christ. No, it's not, it can't be."

Judy had turned to her and waited.

"Do you want me to carry on, what do you want me to do?"

"Oh, erm. I – no, don't."

For a long moment there was silence, the fan on the computer chimed on and off but neither woman spoke.

"We have to, don't we? We just have to. Go on, Judy."

"Are you sure?"

"No, I'm not." Mary reached and grabbed the other woman's hand and then nodded.

Judy turned to the machine and re-activated the video. They observed in silence as the scene changed from the background of curtains and wallpaper and then down to a dishevelled and tumbled bed with a body partly covered by the bright duvet. Pillows were tossed and disturbed and the body was obviously naked. As the view zoomed in, Mary's grip on Judy's hand tightened and she forced her eyes to remain open as the sweep of the camera focused on the face, her face, and then down over her sleeping and unknowing body. A hand came into the scene flicking aside the bedding and there filling the screen was her nakedness, her arms thrown aside in sleep, her breasts slightly squashed against the mattress.

"Turn it off, oh please quickly turn it off."

Judy flicked the screen to darkness and then leaned over and grabbed hold of the shuddering, shaking body beside her.

"I don't need to ask you whether or not you knew about this, do I?"

The horror of it all had stolen her voice and all that Mary could do was to shake her head as she hid her flaming face against the other girl's shoulder.

Chapter 58

They had watched about three quarters of the film as it traced her figure, closing in on her face and hair, and then following the contours from head to toe as she had slept on in blissful ignorance. Stopping it as they had done, they had no idea how intimate it really became.

"Okay. We need to face this. What do you want to do?"

"Delete it, just delete it. I can't bear it."

"Look, Mary you know that deleting this is no answer at all. First of all, this is only a copy from Jacob's machine. So, no matter what we do here with this, the original is still on his laptop and of course probably on his camera. You know this don't you?"

Mary nodded miserably.

"But you could go couldn't you, and delete it, you could get back into his room and just wipe it out? Would you do that for me, could you?"

"Yes, I could and of course I would, but…" Judy took a deep breath. "This video is going to be in at least two other places, Mary. If I wipe it from the folder on his computer, it will still be on the camera and he must have a backup in other places. No, you have got to face this head on. You either go to the police now and tell them what he has done – they may be able and willing to take some action, but I think is probably unlikely given that at the time he made the thing you were in a relationship – or, you have just got to accept that it exists and he can do whatever he likes with it."

Mary gasped and shook her head, panic flared in her eyes.

"There is another option of course."

"What, what other option?"

"Well, you could meet him, you could tell him what we've done and in return for not putting out the pictures of you and Chloe you could ask him to destroy the video. That would mean that your plan will be ruined of course. We won't be able to carry on once he knows we have accessed his laptop and it does put you, well us really, in the wrong. It stinks, but once someone has something like this there is very, very little you can do except hope that they don't put it up on the internet."

"Oh my God, you don't think he would do that do you? Oh no, I couldn't bear it. No, we have to go and get his laptop, we have to smash it, then he won't be able to access the file."

"No, no I'm sorry Mary but that's just not the way it is anymore. He may well have backup copies on memory sticks or even in a cloud. You have to accept that this exists now probably in several different places. It changes the game completely, do you see? If we now publish his work the way we were going to then he can use the video of you as revenge. To put it bluntly, I think that we are screwed."

For several minutes neither of them spoke. Judy because she didn't have anything more to contribute, and Mary because her mind was reeling. She had believed that her clever plan was going to exact revenge and give her back her life and yet again everything had crumbled around her. It was impossible to hold onto coherent thinking as she was lost in a deep panic.

The light had faded and in the quiet living room the only illumination was from the screen, and as the machine went into sleep mode even that was lost. The sudden dimness roused Mary and she stood to pull the drapes over the window and switch on the table lamps. Moving in a daze through what felt like another reality, nothing made sense to her and the image of her naked body was a ghost in the corner of her mind. She flopped onto the settee and raised her gaze to Judy who was still in the swivel chair at the desk.

"What should I do, Judy? Tell me what I should do."

"I don't see that you have a great deal of choice to be frank. I think that you are going to have to speak to him. You're going to have to ask him to delete it. If you don't then you will have to accept that it is out there. Of course, you could brazen it out. How many people do you know who are likely to see it in reality? Then again if we upset him, he might send it to your work. I'm sorry, I don't want to upset you but all of this is possible and it's better to acknowledge what you are dealing with rather than think you have it sorted and then one day – boom – it's all over your screen and people are ringing you up with false sympathy and giggling behind your back.

"You know he may have taken this and had no real intention of using it for anything other than his own pleasure." Mary gasped. "I know, I know even that's horrible but it could just be that he liked being with you so much he wanted to be able to sort of remind himself…" Judy stopped. "No, actually thinking about it, that's grim, if he had asked you that would have been one thing but the fact that you didn't know about it doesn't bode well I have to say. Oh dear, Mary, none of the options are very appealing, are they? You are going to have to tough this out one way or the other. Risk it being seen by people who know you or meet with him and come clean and ask him to delete it."

Mary lowered her head into her hands. He had her in a strangle hold, and yet again, he was impacting on her life in a way she could never have dreamed possible.

She had no idea at all how to react. Her brain was numb.

Chapter 59

"Mary, I'm sorry but I'm going to have to go. I'm meeting Steve. Will you be okay do you think? Is there anyone you can call?"

"No, I'd rather be on my own thanks."

"But, look I really don't want to leave you. It's no good though trying to make a decision about all of this in a rush. I'm really bummed, I thought we could have got this thing on the way tonight and then by tomorrow the shit would have hit the whirly thing and he would have been on the way out of here soon afterwards. Now though, well…" She shrugged her shoulders.

Mary leaned and took hold of the slender hand.

"I can't thank you enough for what you've done, and you know, you have probably saved me from another horrible experience."

"How do you mean?"

"Well, we don't know why he wanted that video in the first place. The thing is though, with the situation we've got now, who knows what he might do. At least now if the worst comes to the worst it won't be out of the blue."

"Yes, I suppose there is that."

With a sigh Judy leaned over and threw her arms around Mary's shoulders in a warm hug. She collected her bag and stood in front of the settee.

"Try not to be too upset. God listen to me, that's stupid. Of course, you're going to be upset. Look I have lectures in the morning but tomorrow afternoon I'll come back and, in the meantime, see if you can come up with some ideas about what you'd like to do. I will call Chloe and tell her that there's been a delay."

Mary walked with her to the door and then locked and bolted it. She unplugged the phone from the wall and, after checking the rest of her security, dragged herself upstairs.

She pulled a clean, fluffy towel from the airing cupboard and then went through to the bedroom, dragged off her clothes and wrapped herself in a robe. As the hot tap gushed into the tub, she poured in bubble bath, turned off the main light and held the lighter to a row of little candles where they stood in glass holders on the shiny ceramic. Once the bath was full of fragrant water and the room was a dim cave of dancing golden light, she lowered herself into the welcoming warmth. She lay her head back and breathed in the perfumed steam. She had to keep control, had to get this in perspective, and then the answer would surely present itself, wouldn't it?

In the street outside evening slid into night. A dark figure walked quickly along the pavement. He clung closely to the garden walls and moved swiftly past the streetlamps. His head was covered by the hood from his jacket and all that could be seen clearly was the reflective flash on his trainers. As he reached Mary's driveway, he left the clangy gate as it was and threw his long legs over the wall. Once in the garden he strode rapidly across the grass and pushed between the shrubs to make his way down the side passageway.

He drew a long screwdriver from his jeans pocket and made short work of opening the back gate. The feeble lock was no match for his strength and determination and in no time, he had access to the back garden. He pushed the gate closed behind him and took the few short steps to the kitchen window. The window was closed completely and the little latch had been pushed home but it was old and the bottom rail fitted loosely in the frame. He took care not to make too much noise.

It took several minutes to push the blade of his tool into the rotting wood but then it was easy to wedge it beneath the catch. He pushed his fingers into the small gap and heaved, and the window slid up with a slight judder. There was a set of garden furniture on the paved patio and he used one of the little chairs to give him the extra height he needed to climb over the sill and access the kitchen.

He knew this room well. He avoided the kettle and toaster, which stood in their usual places on the work top, as he dropped lightly to the floor. From a hip pocket he drew a tiny mag light and following the bright beam made his way to the hallway. He listened closely. From the upper floors the small sounds of water swishing and the hint of perfume that had permeated the hall and stairs told him that she was probably in the bath. The thought of her soaking in the warm water, possibly with bubbles sliding across her skin, gathering around her breasts and nudging at the small swell of her belly caused his breathing to sharpen. He reached out and laid his hand on the balustrade. He took the first silent step onto the staircase.

Mary lay in the comfort of her bathtub breathing deeply, dredging up from her memory the breathing exercises she had learned in relaxation classes many years before. She lay in the candlelight, almost dozing.

Chapter 60

She felt better as the steam, the warmth and peace smoothed the tension from her knotted muscles. Simply lying with eyes closed and letting it all drift away, had worked a small miracle. Stepping from the bath she wrapped the fluffy white towel around her. She felt relaxed and pampered and yes, almost normal.

The problems tried to elbow their way back into the front of her mind and she left her consciousness to slide past them. *I'll think about it later.*

The landing wouldn't be cold but after the blissful heat of the bathroom she knew there would be a chill. She drew open the door and set off across the dim space, scuttling in baby steps.

It was too dark.

She glanced back, the tiny red glow of light on the electric shower witnessed that there was still power in the house but it was so very dark. The diffuse glow of the street outside through the landing window was the only hint of illumination. Why had she closed the bedroom door? She never did that, even when she slept it was slightly ajar and certainly it should be open now. The yellow glow of the bedside lamp ought to be leading her back.

Gripped by confusion and indecision she stood in the middle of the landing trying to remember. Still woozy from her bath and coming down now from the high emotion of earlier, it was difficult to think logically. She shook her head and tried to get herself together.

She shrugged, for some reason she had closed her bedroom door. No matter. Two more steps were all it took and she reached out and pushed at the white painted wood.

The light welcomed her as she knew it would. The smell was the first thing that alerted her, even before she stepped through the door. She knew it immediately, his cologne. It took her breath away; it was a memory surely, a sense of deja vu.

It wasn't.

He was sitting on the bed. As her eyes met his and her mouth opened in a gasp, he raised his hands, palms towards her and braced his legs to stand.

"Don't panic, please Mary, don't panic. You don't need to be afraid."

Fear wasn't even close to describing what she felt. The world tipped, and colours blurred but she had to stay conscious, had to save herself. She didn't speak, couldn't speak, fear made her dumb. She clung to the towel, tightening it around her goose skin. She held her body upright, though it wanted to crumble to the floor. She denied the urging of her brain which so badly wanted to take her away. She didn't faint but locked her knees and held his gaze. Each thing a tiny victory, each victory a step back from total meltdown.

"I just need to speak to you, Mary. I've tried to call, I left messages, I tried to see you. I want to explain, to apologise. I know it was unforgivable, what I did, I'm so sorry."

He had come to her. She could feel his breath on her face as he leaned nearer, could see the glint in his eye, a tear just a moment away from overflowing. His lips quivered. His hand reached out. His touch was searing. She would scream, she must scream, it was impossible. She snatched breath into her lungs and that was the most that she could accomplish.

"Come on, sit down. Here, put your dressing gown on."

He opened her wardrobe. The hook was empty, her robe still on the bathroom floor, but how well he knew her, her home, her life.

"Oh, wait, wait, I'll fetch it. You're shivering, you're cold." He pushed past her. Now she could run, but was frozen to the spot. Her legs would not obey the messages from her brain.

She could hear him in the other room and stood still waiting for whatever would come next.

Chapter 61

"Here, here. Oh, you poor thing you're shivering."

He draped the fluffy dressing gown across her shoulders and then, stepping round to face her, pulled it across her chest and belly. As he did this, he placed his fingers on the towel still clutched with claw-like hands over her damp skin. "This is wet, let me take it."

"No, no. Don't please, Jacob don't touch me." The feel of his hands released her from the strange terror driven fugue. "I'm okay."

She pulled the robe across tight to her body, the towel was tucked inside and as she tied the belt the heavy, damp cloth fell to the floor. Jacob was still close and she stepped away further into the room. Her heart pounded but the initial fear had dissipated. She swung round to him and looked him in the eye, holding his gaze.

"I want you to go now, Jacob. I want you to just leave right now."

"Mary, Mary," he said and reached a hand towards her, "now, I know you're upset, and I suppose really I don't blame you but when you give me a chance to talk to you and explain, you'll see, you'll understand."

She shook her head vigorously.

"I don't want to hear it. I don't even want to talk to you. I just want you to leave, please now, go."

Still he didn't turn but continued to look at her, his head tipped to one side and a half smile playing about his lips.

"Look, let's just sit down. Let's have a cup of tea and talk things over. There's no need for any of this. You'll see we can sort it out."

He took hold of her arm and tried to pull her with him towards the door. She attempted to shake him off and his grip tightened. The fear was back, the feel of his strong fingers digging into the soft skin of her upper arm was scaring her all over again.

"Let me go, please just let me go!" The muscles of her face tensed as her mouth tightened, a scream was but a breath away. He shook his head again but he did loosen his grip.

"Oh Mary, what can I do, how can I make things right?"

Her jelly legs could hold her no longer and she collapsed onto the edge of the bed. She clutched at the gown where it had begun to gape at the neck.

"You can't make it right, Jacob. There's no way to make it right."

"But I didn't mean to hurt you. Your poor face, you've no idea how it hurts me to see that. Oh, you don't understand, sometimes I just lose it. I know I shouldn't but it's like another person takes over and I just can't help it."

A throb in his voice told her that he too was but a blink away from losing control and the thought of what would happen then terrified her, all that mattered was to get him out of the house.

"Look, Jacob, if you leave right now, I'll let it all go. If you promise not to try and get in touch with me again, and to leave me completely alone I'll just forget it. I won't tell anyone what you did, and I'll just try and put it behind me. Okay?"

"No, no, no. I need you."

He dropped to his knees on the carpet in front of her. His hands reached out to her. She shook him off but was unable to stand.

"Please, oh please. You don't know, you don't understand what you mean to me. You're the first person who ever treated me like you do. I never felt about anyone the way I feel about you. Please, Mary, let's try again."

He had shuffled now towards her and had his arms laid across the bed either side of her quivering thighs.

"Please, don't do this. Don't turn me away. Not you, not you, Lovely Lady. I thought you were different, not like all the other women. Nobody has ever looked at me the way that you did. Nobody made me feel the way that you did. Please."

She tried to shuffle backwards away from him but he held her, his hands curled around her bottom and to her horror he lowered his head onto her lap and sobbed onto her towelling-covered legs.

From somewhere deep inside came the impulse to reach out and to stroke his soft hair, to murmur words of comfort. His tears, the sound of him sobbing, unleashed in her an instinct that was womanly and loving. Female intuition and motherly emotions moved her in a way that she wouldn't have believed possible.

She stretched her fingers and laid her hand across his crown.

Chapter 62

The moment stretched into a minute and then two and once she had placed her hand on his soft hair Mary didn't know how to remove it. He had sobbed for a while but was now simply kneeling at her feet with his face buried in the fluff of her dressing gown. She was vitally aware of nerve endings feeding back messages to her brain. His arms were warm where they touched her thighs and strong hands, curled around her behind, heated her skin through the thick fabric.

Her lungs felt as though they had shrunk to half their size and it seemed incredible that the tiny little gasps she took were dragging in enough oxygen to feed her body's needs. It was not a beautiful moment. She was not swept with feelings of forgiveness or affection. She just wanted it to be over. Panic built, she needed to act and throw him aside, needed him gone and didn't know how to accomplish it.

She drew back her hand and then bracing both beside her on the bed tried to push forward and to stand. As Jacob felt her moving, he raised his head.

"I need to get up, Jacob. I need to dry my hair. Give me some space."

Now he threw up his hands and shuffled backwards.

"Okay, okay. But we're going to have a talk then and I'm going downstairs to put the kettle on. Or perhaps you'd prefer wine, brandy – you choose."

He smiled at her then and the relaxed friendliness frightened her anew. It seemed he had simply put aside the problems, the beating he had given her and all the worry and stress of the last days. He was behaving as though nothing had happened.

She must be strong.

"No, Jacob I don't want to have a drink with you. I don't want a cup of tea. I want you to leave. I don't want you to be here in my house."

"Oh, now, come on that's just silly."

"No, it's not silly. It's what I want. I don't think I can trust you anymore and I don't want to be with you."

"Oh, for heaven's sake. That is such an overreaction you silly girl. Okay, I made a mistake but it was nothing and I promise you that I won't do it again but you know it was partly your fault."

"What!" Shock screwed her voice into a screech and as the sound left her throat, she saw him flinch and then incredibly his face transformed into a smile.

"Oh, now see. You're getting yourself all upset and really there is no need."

"But, how dare you? How can you suggest it was my fault, what the hell do you mean?"

He tipped his head to one side and raised his eyebrows.

"Well, okay if I really have to explain it to you." He sighed. "You let me down, Mary. You really did. I thought that what we had was special. I thought you had genuine feelings for me, and I thought that I could trust you."

"I don't know what you are talking about."

He snorted. "This isn't helping now. You know very well. I heard that message from your mother. You'd been gossiping, hadn't you? First, you'd been talking about me with your friend Jane and then with your mother. Tell me, did you get a buzz out of it, did you have a good giggle?"

The change in tone was small, almost imperceptible but with her instincts in hyper drive Mary picked it up immediately and a cold chill ran down her back.

"Please go Jacob, really there's no point to any of this. It's over and I want you to go."

"Oh, I don't think so. No, do you think that I have no say here? Do you think that you get to call the tune all the time? I really thought you were different, but look at you stood there now telling me what to do. Why is it you women think that you can do this? You think you can pick me up and get what you want. Oh yes, you weren't like this when you were gagging for it were you – no. You didn't tell me to leave you alone while we were rolling about on the mattress next door. I really thought you might be different but turns out you're just like all the others."

He hissed now through his teeth and grabbed out at her arms. She tried to back away but was still too close to the bed and fell backwards across the mattress.

Now he leaned over her.

"Is that what I was to you eh, is it – was I just a good screw, just a toy boy, a bit of a fling?"

"No, no of course not."

She had to get away. The softness that had flooded his eyes just a short while ago had been replaced by a fierce glare. One wrong move and the repercussions would be very dire indeed.

"Okay, okay. Let me dry my hair, you go and make us a cup of tea."

He stood and with a small glance backwards left the room. She pushed the door closed, grabbed up her handbag and rootled inside for her mobile but of course when she found the little device, it refused to fire up. Because it had been kept turned off, to avoid his persistent calls and texts, she had forgotten to keep it charged. "Damn it." She threw it down onto the bed.

Maybe if she could get downstairs without him knowing, she could get through the front door and possibly into the road and run next door. She dragged on a track suit and socks, but her shoes were in the cupboard downstairs. No matter, she would go barefoot if she had to, the main thing was to get away.

The stairs were carpeted and on tiptoe she took the first few nervous steps down. He was in the kitchen running water, clattering in the cupboards. The noise was a blessing covering her progress.

Halfway down she clung to the banister rail and leaned over to peer into the room at the end of the hallway. She couldn't see him. It didn't matter, the front door was within reach, five more steps and she would be in the hall.

Now, now, a flurry and rush and she was there the latch under her quivering hands. She was getting out, getting away. She dragged at the door – *blast it, blast it*, the deadlock was on. She leaned to release the catch.

"What are you doing?"

He was behind her, standing in the kitchen doorway staring down the narrow space. His face was frozen in a frown, and his words were ice. She turned and at once understood that right now at this moment she was in more danger than ever before in her life.

Chapter 63

Never before had Mary truly understood how air could be suffused with threat. She had believed that to be a myth, until now.

Jacob took his hand from the kitchen door frame and straightened. He was coming for her. The door was at her back, the deadlock still fastened. If she took the risk she would be turned from him as he approached. The length of the hallway was perhaps ten steps for a man of his height. How long would that give her?

"Jacob, you're frightening me. You're making me really scared. Stay there, please don't come any closer."

"Where are you going? I have the kettle on. We're going to have a drink and a nice talk. We're going to sort all this out. Why are you trying to run away? Oh, come on, surely that little slap isn't the cause of all this? Anyway I said I was sorry, you know that. Come on now. Come into the kitchen with me."

He had taken two or three steps but no more and now he stood with his hand raised towards her the palm upward in a gesture of supplication.

"Jacob, you need to understand. What you're calling a little slap, what you are dismissing so easily, it was a terrible thing. Surely you know that, you must. No one has ever raised their hand to me. It is never okay to do that. Look, please, just let me go."

"Oh, that's all modern nonsense, Mary. I know we're all supposed to pretend that it doesn't happen but – well – of course it does. My dad – oh look let's not get into that. Let's just say that I know how things really are, in families, between men and women, dads and their kids. I know that sometimes things get a bit silly and at the end of the day someone has to be in charge, it's not rocket science. Someone has to be in control. I trusted you, I thought you cared about me and well, you let me down. So, you see, what else could I do, okay I flew off the handle but it was understandable, wasn't it? All I was doing was making a point."

"No, no that's not right. That's not the way it is. In normal homes, normal relationships, that's not the way it is."

He took the next steps, and shook his head. The heavy fringe that she had so loved flopped into his eyes; he pushed it back across his frowning forehead.

"Look Mary, we can argue about this till the cows come home but we don't need to. Let's just agree that it was all an unfortunate misunderstanding and we'll try not to let it happen again and then we can get back to where we were."

"No, there is no way I can do that. I can't be with someone who is violent. I just can't."

"Me, violent? I'm not violent, don't be ridiculous."

An answer simply would not form in her mouth. As it became clear just how truly disturbed he was, her mind was in turmoil. She could tell him that she knew about Chloe, but how could she? The girl had paid her price. She could ask him why he had filmed her naked while she was sleeping, but then she would be involving Judy. There was nothing more in her arsenal, and she had no way to rescue him from the influences of his past. It was all beyond her, she couldn't cope. She wanted to curl into a ball and howl like a child.

She slid to the floor and lowered her pounding head between bent knees.

He was here. The heat of his body and the smell of him and the sound of him breathing caused her heart to somersault and her stomach to clench. She believed she may throw up from the effects of pure panic. Strong hands wrapped around hers pulling her arms from where they shielded her head.

"Come on now, stand up. Let's stop all this nonsense."

Chapter 64

She began to believe that he wasn't going to hurt her, not now. Perhaps the moment of danger had passed.

He held her to him, his strength was comforting. His mouth teased at the lobe of an ear and tracked down now brushing her neck. Hands stroked her back as his lips found hers, soft and searching and oh so wonderful. As she felt the warmth of his kiss gentling her mouth, quisling instincts softened her lips and parted them to the heat of his passion. The stress and tension of the last days had made her weak, she craved solace. It would be the easiest thing in the world to lean against him and surrender to the moment, the bliss and the beauty; to let go of all the worry and just be with him.

The kiss became more urgent, his embrace tightened, and in a blink, the moment shattered. Mary panicked. What was she thinking? He had struck her, betrayed her and could not be trusted, there was no way that this should be happening. It must not be allowed. She tried to twist her face away from his and to squirm out of the circle of his arms.

"Oh, for heaven's sake. You stupid woman." He had leaned back, just a little and now glared at her with eyes hardened by impatience. "What is the matter with you? For Pete's sake."

"Let me go, just let me go and get out of my house. I don't trust you. I don't want you in my life anymore."

The bravery was formed partly of panic and partly of anger at herself for the brief instant of weakness. Her voice was shrill and from somewhere came the strength to push him backwards and twist away from his grip.

It was a small victory, but the door was still at her back and his bulk blocked any hope she had of gaining the relative freedom of the hallway.

They were locked in a moment of high tension. He would not move and she could not. Mary didn't dare to speak, and Jacob shook his head in frustration. He breathed heavily, snorting air through his nostrils, the tender lips had hardened now into a thin line. She was terribly aware of the change in his demeanour. As his arms withdrew, she saw his fists clench, the fire in his eyes deepened to a blaze of anger.

She had to get away and escape this mounting fury. A small step to the side may give her a chance to duck away from him and to run, but as she made the attempt, he simply stretched his arms wider and barred her way.

He was looking at her now puzzlement drawing lines on his brow. He rocked back on his heels and again shook his head.

"It's amazing how wrong you can be, isn't it? Lovely lady, that's what you were to me. I thought you were real and now look. There's nothing lovely about you, is there, Mary? You're just another traitorous bloody female. I don't know why I bother you know. I keep falling for it, making a fool of myself; keep giving myself and every time, every time this happens."

As he spoke, his voice rose in power and tempo until now he was screaming at her. He drew back his arm and launched his fist inches above her head. "Damn it, damn it."

Mary screamed as the stud wall rattled under the force of his blow.

"Oh shut up, just shut up." He reached now, too quickly for her to dodge and grabbed her shoulder. "Listen to you squealing and carrying on. I didn't hurt you did I, did I?"

She tried to speak but terror had stolen her voice and so she shook her head.

"No, no, see it's all in your mind, all of this. It's you, isn't it?" He bent, his face an inch from hers and she felt the spray of saliva as he hissed at her.

"I'm sorry," she managed to whisper.

"What, what did you say?"

"I'm sorry."

"Sorry, oh now you're sorry. Now you've spoiled everything, now you've done this, made me so angry – now you're sorry."

She nodded and then gasped as his hand found her throat. He had her now backed against the wall, his breath hot on her face. One hand was resting against the damaged wall the other tightening the grip on her neck, cutting off her ability to breathe.

"Christ. Bloody hell, Mary!"

The scream came from somewhere outside of this tiny circle of horror. She knew the voice but not how it could be here. As he tightened his grip yet more, she thought her mind had played a trick. Darkness hovered at the edge of her mind then she saw him turn and a blessed relaxation of his hold on her allowed precious air into her screaming lungs. The darkness receded and she could hear the yelling again, clearer now and real.

"Jacob, what are you doing? Let her go, let her go!"

He spun around as a whirling, screeching dervish threw herself at him clawing and yelling and thumping. Mary slid down the wall as Jacob raised his hands to protect himself from the slapping and thumping that Judy was delivering to his face and head.

"What the hell are you doing here, Judy? Look this is nothing to do with you, this is between me and Mary. Anyway, where did you come from? Shit stop it, stop it."

Judy reached out and snatched up a lamp from the hall table. She came towards him swinging the heavy metal, screaming and landing blow after blow on Jacob's shoulders and arms. If she had been strong enough to heft the lamp at his head, then the consequences would have been more devastating but as it was, he whirled away from her and ran through the hallway.

Judy dropped to the carpet and threw her arms around the shaking and sobbing figure of Mary and they heard him rattling the locks and flinging the door back on its hinges. As she rocked the other woman, gently crooning words of comfort, heavy footsteps pounded up the drive and then there came the rattle of the gate.

"How are you here? Where did you come from?" Mary's voice was ragged, through the sobbing and gasping.

She clutched at Judy who helped her up and led her slowly into the living room where she wrapped a throw around the shaking shoulders and then sat beside her on the settee holding her close and rocking her gently.

"I was worried about you and so I came back and when I saw that the side gate was open, I knew something was wrong. I went round to the kitchen. The window was open and I could hear the yelling, so I climbed in. God Mary, what the hell are you going to do now?"

Chapter 65

There was no question of going to bed. Mary wondered if she would ever sleep again. She could still feel the shadow of his hand around her neck and the ghastly choking feeling that had tightened her throat.

"Can you stay, Judy? I know it's a lot to ask but can you stay with me tonight? I don't want to be on my own."

"I wouldn't dream of going anywhere else."

"You can use the guest room, if you're tired. I'm going to sit here for a while." Her voice quivered and Judy leaned to her again and squeezed her shoulders.

"Or, we could work on the programme."

Mary was motionless, barely breathing, staring into the dimly lit room. After a minute she gulped.

"We could, couldn't we? Judy do you think that's what we should do?"

"Well, you don't want to call the police?"

Mary shook her head.

"No, I couldn't bear it. The fuss and the embarrassment, everyone knowing. I know that maybe I should but I just can't. I think it would just make it all so much worse."

"Well, in that case it's back to square one isn't it? Drive him out, disgrace him and if possible, screw up his degree submission. It's just about ready you know. If we get to it now, we can finish it in a couple of hours and then by morning it could be out there."

"What about Chloe?"

"I'll send her a text but really there isn't going to be too much for her to worry about. I don't think anyone will know who she is. Unless you were here at the time and were close to her it would be very difficult to piece it together and there are only a couple of us who know what happened and we're going to protect her as best we can."

"Ok, yes."

"You though, well, you're still here. There are a few people at the house who know that you and Jacob had a thing going on. Some of them guessed about your relationship and they are going to know. I don't think there's any way to avoid it. We can blank out your eyes and so on but I think you have to be prepared for the fact that people will guess. You say you don't want the police here because it'll all become common knowledge but you know, it's going to be out there even if we do it this way."

"Yes, yes, I know. I did hope that we could do this without revealing who I was but I realised a while ago that it probably wasn't going to be possible. The thing is though, doing it this way I don't have to convince anyone. You were here tonight. You saw my face before; what he did. I don't have to stand in front of a judge and tell a jury what he did and hope they believe me. I know if it came to that I'd wimp out. I know they'd look at me and think I was a desperate middle-aged woman throwing herself at a young man. He is lovely-looking you have to admit. He is handsome and he seems kind. That's one of the worst things about all this you know. He is kind, and gentle and funny."

She started to sob, and Judy sat beside her holding her hand while she allowed the tears to drip down her cheeks.

"Let's do it, let's just see if this can work and then maybe I can have my life back."

They powered up the computer and polished and tweaked the damning evidence ready to launch it on the college Intranet the next morning. Mary dragged herself into the kitchen to make them hot chocolate and toast which she then couldn't eat because of the soreness in her throat.

As the dawn crept across the sky, and the birds argued and gossiped in the trees outside, they pressed the key. Such a small action. They hugged, a warm, sisterly embrace and then settled down, Judy in the big armchair and Mary on the couch. They covered themselves with duvets and they waited.

Chapter 66

The smell of toast and coffee dragged Mary from her sleep. She felt stiff and sore, her throat hurt and there was a deep, shocked sadness like a lump of cold dough in her chest.

Judy was busy in the kitchen and the radio played quietly in the background. She threw the duvet to the floor and creaked and groaned her way to the breakfast table.

"How are you? I hope you don't mind, I made us some coffee and toast or would you rather have tea?"

"No, coffee's brilliant. Thanks so much, there's jam in the fridge."

"Right, so how are you feeling?"

"I don't know to be honest. I ache a bit and my throat hurts when I swallow but I just feel so sad. It's like someone came and stole all the light and colour from my life. I just feel sort of grey, I can't think of any other way to put it."

"Hey, you need to be strong, Mary. You can't let yourself drift into depression; if you do, he's done even more damage to you. It's going to be over soon, and you can box it away. I know you won't forget but you can make it part of your history. But you mustn't let it define who you are, don't become a victim."

"How did you get to be so wise?"

"Well, to be honest there is history in my family of this sort of thing. I don't intend to talk about it and it wasn't personal but I've seen it before and you have to be strong."

"Is that why you came to see me, because of your family?"

"Partly yes, I admit that when I saw you with him, I felt obliged to warn you. I didn't do a very good job of it in the end did I?"

"You did what you could and I'll always be grateful. I think if you hadn't come along last night, he might actually have killed me you know."

As the words left her mouth Mary felt her fingers start to shake and she wrapped them around the warmth of the coffee mug to still the quivering.

"I have never come across anything like this. Oh yes at work I've seen people who have been beaten, women with black eyes and bruises, but I would never have believed it could happen to me. My husband could no more have hit me, or anyone for that matter, than fly.

"It has made me look at so many things differently. I realise now how precious it is to have peace and security, how just living an ordinary life can actually be enough. On top of that though it's made me maybe want to do something, you know maybe see if I can help other people."

"I can give you some numbers if you like? I have contacts at some of the women's refuges."

"That'd be great. When this is all over, I'll have a word with someone.

"Judy, do you know, what makes them do it? Do you have any idea why someone like Jacob could be so lovely and kind and gentle one minute and then a brutal fiend the next?"

Judy shook her head. "It's not simple and I think that there are lots of reasons. I think that if children are beaten and mistreated, they do often go on to do it themselves as adults but it's very complicated. I have read some stuff about it but I think each case has to be judged individually."

"I just wonder you know, if anything could be done – for Jacob."

As she sat down with a plate of toast in one hand and her own coffee in the other, Judy shrugged.

"He'd need to either want to find help or, heaven forbid, hurt someone so badly that the police became involved, and they would make him have treatment I think."

"What will be happening now, with the website?"

"Hmmm, let's see, it's eight o'clock. The first of his pictures will be going live in half an hour. Then it will pretty much depend on whether he sees it himself or someone tells him. There is the outside chance that if he sees the first couple he will get in touch with IT and get them to investigate. He could possibly have the thing stopped if there is anyone there bright enough to get to it. I'm hoping though that by the time he finds out, enough of his degree work will have been published for it to mean he's no chance of replacing it and then, at two o'clock this afternoon the pictures of you and Chloe will be up. That's when it's busiest, as people come back from lunch and they want to check mail and so on.

"I did it that way so that interest will build through the day, we could have put it all up together one image after the other quickly, but then a lot of people might not have seen it. What will happen now is that during the day anyone on the computers will suddenly find their screen filled with one after the other of his pictures and then this afternoon ours. By just after two o'clock it will be done Mary, and then we just have to wait and see what happens."

"The college might take action, he could just make a run for it, or the others might be so shocked that they force him to leave. It was a great plan but we can't be absolutely sure of the outcome. I hope the college chuck him out but..." she shrugged.

"I thought that I'd go in this morning to the college and see what sort of reaction there is and then come back here to be with you later. We can watch it live if you can bear it or just wait until something happens. It's up to you."

"I'm going to have to ring work this morning and tell them I'll be back next week and then I'm going to clean the house, top to bottom. I'm going to keep busy, keep my mind occupied. I think I'd want to watch it go live and then I'll know it's happened."

"Right." Judy gulped back the last of her drink and then pulled on her coat. She leaned and kissed Mary on the cheek. "Be strong Mary, it's nearly over."

The kindness almost overwhelmed her but she straightened her shoulders and walked to the front door to take off the locks and then reinstate the security after the other woman had left. A long morning stretched before her but she felt a stirring of an odd excitement.

Chapter 67

Mary's stomach was tied in knots. In just a few minutes the photographs of her battered and bruised face would pop up on all the "in use" computers at the college. It was the middle of the afternoon. Judy had remarked that just then almost every computer would be in use.

When Judy returned from her morning lectures, she reported that the publication of Jacob's degree show images on the college intranet was causing a furore. Most people were incensed, she said.

"Nearly everyone has assumed that it's a rotten trick by someone who is jealous of his skill and so he has a great deal of sympathy."

Mary covered her mouth with her hands.

"That's not what was supposed to happen. I didn't think that would be what happened."

"No, no it's exactly what should happen. Up to now no one knows what it's all about and so he is a bit of a hero — once the other pictures come up those people who have come out on his side will be thrown into turmoil. They won't approve of what he's done and they are going to hate the fact that by association he has put them in the wrong camp. Really, it's fine Mary, it's what I expected."

"Has he said anything?"

"No, nobody has seen him. He's not at the house and none of his friends have seen him at the college. He could be out on an assignment, but wherever he is there is a nasty surprise waiting for him when he comes back."

They settled themselves in front of the computer desk, booted up and counted down the minutes.

When the first of the photographs popped up Mary found her response to be flat and unemotional. She had known what her face looked like, had watched the swelling decrease and the bruising fade from livid purple to black through to yellow. Seeing it now on the screen it felt as though she was looking at a photograph of someone else. The images of Chloe shocked her more. The damage seemed a greater outrage on the younger, prettier face, though she knew that it was no such thing.

There were six images in total and between each one the text, 'And this is the work of Jacob Chadwick. Is this a man you want to call friend?' in flashing red letters which slowly faded into the next horrible image. Judy had done a brilliant job.

Even before the last picture flashed onto the screen Judy's phone began to chirp and tinkle, text messages and emails flooded in from friends and class-mates. She scrolled quickly through them reading out excerpts here and there. Of course, they didn't know of her involvement and so many of them simply told her what was going on and then commented on their reactions.

'What a monster, who are these women?'

'No, this can't be true.'

'Who put this show up? I want to shake them by the hand.'

'What proof is there that this is genuine?'

And of course, 'Where is Jacob, has anyone seen him, what does he say about it?'

Judy pushed back from the desk and turned to Mary who was staring dried eyed and silent at the screen.

This wasn't how she had expected people to react. All she felt was drained and emptied out. It had taken a lot of arranging from the first germ of a plan and now with no real idea of what was coming next it all seemed an anti-climax.

"You okay, Mary?" In response to Judy's quiet question she just nodded. How strange was this? She had expected a sort of euphoria and all there was really was a deep sadness and a feeling that something precious had been lost to her.

"You did a brilliant job, Judy. Thank you."

"Mary, this is only the start, we have to wait now. That was only the touch paper, we lit it and now we have to wait for the fireworks, don't we?"

"Yes, yes of course you're right. I wonder where he is though. I wonder if he's seen it yet, or maybe someone has told him. You'll think I'm mad but I feel sorry for him."

"I know, I know… Hell, Mary haven't you got any alcohol in this place? This is time for a drink, a big drink. If you like, I'll stay with you. I've told Steve I probably can't see him tonight. We could send out for a pizza, maybe, or something. We need to lift your mood and we deserve a celebration, at the very least it was damned good hacking."

She laughed and raised her hand palm facing Mary and they high fived and then fell onto each other in a hug.

"You are amazing, Judy. You really are."

"Yeah well – if you say so. Now about that drink."

As she uncorked the bottle of wine Mary couldn't shake an awful premonition that she hadn't yet seen the worst of it. Somewhere a foreshadowing told her what was to come next would be shattering and would change her life forever. She didn't believe in premonitions but this feeling was so very strong it was as if the very air she breathed knew about it and wanted to warn her.

She told herself it was a reaction. It was an adrenalin withdrawal after a period of stress, a trick of her overwrought brain but no matter what she told herself it felt real and no amount of red wine and pizza was going to chase it away. She caught a glance of her face reflected in the kitchen window. A pale wraith-like creature looked back at her, a creature who had seen the future and knew the horrors that it held.

Chapter 68

Judy had been gone for a couple of hours, and the house was calm and tidy again. Mary peered at her reflection in the hall mirror. Another couple of days and she could probably risk a visit to her mum and dad. The bruises were fading fast and could soon be covered by foundation and concealer. It was a long time since she'd seen her parents and guilt had started to wheedle its way in. She felt the now familiar prickle of tears in the corners of her eyes. Would the crying ever stop?

So much had happened since she was last in their little bungalow and a lot of the drama hinged on the call her mum had made. Of course, they were never to know anything about all of this. She would cut out her tongue before she told them of the torment she had endured, and she would go to any and all lengths to avoid her mum feeling guilty because of her words on the telephone. Yes, by the end of the week she would go to see them and maybe take them out to lunch. It would be lovely to do something normal, something that felt like old times.

With a jolt of shock, she realised that the house phone had been unplugged since before the horrible night when Jacob had tried to strangle her. She flew down the hall, yes, there was the tiny plug lying on the carpet. Her mobile was off as well, if her mum and dad had been trying to contact her at all over the last couple of days, they would be worried sick. She would have to ring them.

She stuck the little plastic plug back into the socket and lifted the receiver, why she did that she couldn't have said but in the event the purring of the dial tone was reassuring, being as it was a connection with life outside of the house and her problems.

She glanced around. There was no mark on the wall, no blood on the carpet, nothing to witness the horrible events of two nights ago. Would she ever truly be able to forget, to move on and enjoy her home the way she had before? Doubts were creeping in and ironically the steps she had taken to protect the status quo had led her to think that it wasn't what she wanted after all.

She replaced the handset and it rang before she had a chance to move more than a couple of steps away. Jacob didn't have this number, so it was alright to answer.

"Hello."

"Mary, it's Judy. Are you okay?"

"Hi. Yes, I'm okay."

"Are you really, is there anyone there with you?"

"No, I'm on my own. I was just going to go to the shops."

"Honestly?"

"Yes, Judy what's the matter?"

"Oh, I'm probably just being silly. Nobody has seen Jacob. He didn't go back to the house last night. Steve rang me this morning. He wanted to talk about yesterday of course. Anyway, it seems that Jacob was out early yesterday morning and nobody has seen him since then. We don't know if he has seen the pictures and already made a run for it, though that seems unlikely as his stuff is all still there. The boys at the house are wondering what to do. They don't know whether they should tell the college, or just wait. They've tried ringing him and his phone's off.

I was really calling to make sure he wasn't there and to warn you."

"Oh. I don't know what to say, Judy. I don't know what to do. I haven't been out yet today but I've had no trouble here. I suppose it would be best if they report it. I suppose it is unusual for him not to come home isn't it?"

"Well yes but it is just one night. The college is buzzing with reaction to the pictures yesterday, the authorities obviously know about it. I suppose we'll just have to wait and see what happens next. Look make sure you lock your doors and windows – better still can't you go and stay with someone, you know, just get away from there for now?"

"I don't know, I suppose I could but…"

"Look just be careful yeah. I'll call you again if I hear anything. Do you think you could bear to put your mobile on? There is the risk that he'll call you or text but anyway, I think you should make sure you can be reached."

"I will. Thanks, Judy. I'm going out now for about an hour. I'll be okay. Don't worry."

"Mary, take care."

A quiver of fear ran through her body, a board somewhere in the house clicked as it cooled and her heart pounded, every nerve ending jumped as if she'd touched a live wire.

Where was he?

Chapter 69

Jane. Jane was the answer, well maybe. Mary wanted to try and sort things out anyway and perhaps now, when she truly needed a friend and a safe haven, this was the time. She had read somewhere that if you want to make someone your friend then ask a favour of them. Jane had long been her friend, until the recent falling out anyway, and so perhaps this was an ideal way to get back in touch.

She picked up the telephone handset.

"Hi, Jane. It's me. It's Mary."

"Oh. Hi. How are you?"

"Not that brilliant actually."

"Oh, oh right, well I'm sorry to hear that. Can I do anything, are you ill?"

"Not exactly but I'm in a hell of mess, Jane."

Mary was surprised to hear her own words were shaky and her voice cracked. She had intended to be calm, strong, but the sound of the familiar voice undid her shattered nerves.

"Oh love." And there it was. The depth of their friendship swam to the surface and in an instant, all was resolved.

"Oh Jane, I've been such a fool and you were right and, well it's been dreadful and now I'm very scared."

"Scared?"

"Yes, I think I may be in danger. Look I don't want to talk about it over the phone. Can I come over to your house, and Jane, could I stay with you tonight?"

"Of course you can. Get yourself here right now. I'll shift the car so you have room to park. Just pull in behind me on the drive. See you in about half an hour, yeah?"

"It'll take me a bit longer. I need to pack a couple of things and lock up. Jane, thanks."

"I'm waiting for you love."

She threw her overnight things into a bag, watered her plants and packed the perishables from the fridge into an insulated bag to take with her. She chose a couple of bottles of wine from the rack and dumped the whole lot into the car. Once the house was locked and bolted, she left without even a backward glance. Reaching the end of the road a wave of relief swept over her. Her heart lifted as she let go the fear that had wrapped around it like a string of barbs. It was all spoiled wasn't it, her home, her life, her peace? Everything of value was gone and she didn't see how it could be regained. The love that had made the place special had been overtaken by fear, pain and ugliness.

Passing the bus stop where the whole sorry affair had started, she glanced at the small queue. Of course he wasn't there but if he had been then it wouldn't have surprised her. In her mind he was always there, bright hair shining in the sunshine, mouth curved in a gentle smile and his eyes glinting with amusement.

The drive was uneventful and as she turned into the narrow driveway Jane opened the door and hurried forward to help with the bags. Once inside they held each other for a long time. There were hugs and smiles and comforting warmth. Jane offered tea but they decided to open the wine; Jane in celebration at the return of her friend and Mary because she needed the boost to her courage. Each of them still stood in different landscapes but now Mary was to pull Jane across the divide as she revealed the turmoil that her life had become. They settled in her bright dining room and for a long moment there was quiet as Mary searched for the words to start the difficult conversation.

Once she started it all spilled out easily. Jane reached across the shining tabletop and laid her hand on top of Mary's, her eyes glittered with moisture but she didn't speak until it was over.

"So, where is he now?"

"Nobody knows. He hasn't been seen since yesterday."

"Well, you're safe here anyway, but why haven't you called the police? Surely that's what you should do."

"Oh Jane, you were right before and you're probably right now but it's all too late. I've got it all wrong from the start and I just don't know what I can do to fix it. I think I'm going to have to sell the house and move away. It's just not the same anymore, all the memories of Bill, the things we did, the happiness, it's been obliterated, I just can't find it anymore. I think that's one of the worst things you know. I feel that I let him down, Bill."

Now was the 'I told you so moment' but it didn't happen and the fact that she simply squeezed Mary's hand and then took a big swig of her white wine was more precious than gold to Mary and wiped away any residual ill feeling between them.

"You can stay here as long as you want to. Does your friend Judy know where you are?

"No, I'll call her and let her know. Right now, though, I would love to just sit here with you in this room and wipe it all out. I wish I could erase the whole thing but I can't."

"No, you can't but you can move on, I'll help you. This isn't the end of the world, Mary. It's a glitch and no matter what you decide to do, about your house and all of that, I'll help you. It's going to be fine."

Mary's phone chimed and the text alert blinked at her. For a moment her finger hovered over the answer key but the peace was so very precious that she rejected the call and turned off her mobile without even glancing at the screen and the tiny scroll of words.

235

Chapter 70

Although the problems were still there, Mary felt soothed after spending time with her old friend. They talked for hours about Jacob and about the abortive lunch date which had ended in bitterness and ill feeling. They laughed also, about good times, and Mary was surprised to find herself with a smile on her face and lightness in her soul that had for a time seemed unreachable.

"I've put you in Millie's room and Alan is away on business so it's just us, at least until the weekend if you want to stay that long."

"I don't know, love, perhaps tomorrow. A lot of it depends on what happens with him, Jacob. If the college throw him out and he goes quickly then I can safely return home. I have a horrible feeling that if I stay away too long it might be impossible to go back, even now when I think about it, I feel sick. I'm going to have to sell it aren't I?"

"Hey, give it time, wait a while. You've always loved the place. Don't do anything rash."

"Oh, I don't know, perhaps it's a good thing. Maybe I should make more effort. One thing that I have learned from all of this is that I had become very set in my ways. I had a lovely unchallenging rut and maybe I was just a bit too comfortable with it, wasting my opportunities or not even looking for them. I mean, I'm not that old and when I look at it all from a different perspective well – another twenty, thirty years just living from day to day it's a waste isn't it?"

Jane shrugged her shoulders and raised her eyebrows. They ate and had another couple of drinks, they listened to some music. It was calm and wonderful.

"I think I'm ready to call it a day if that's okay, can I go up? Millie's room yeah?"

"Yes, go on up. I'll just do the lights, check the doors and stuff. I've put you a towel in there. If you need anything let me know."

Mary closed the door to the little bedroom, there were posters on the wall, and a collection of well-loved teddies gazed down indifferently from a shelf above the desk. Millie had been away at University for two years now and it was ages since they had done anything together. That was another area of her life that she would have to sort out.

As she snuggled beneath the covers. She wanted to set an alarm for the morning and so she reached into her handbag for her mobile and turned it on.

It tinkled and dinged, moving through the boot sequence, but then there were more alert tones. She had forgotten about the text message which had come in earlier. It would be easier to leave it until tomorrow. If it was from Jacob, she wouldn't read it anyway, just delete it the same as all the others. With a sigh she clicked into the message field.

The first one had his name on it. Her finger hovered over the button. He was no longer her problem. Was he? There was one from Judy, asking if she was okay and with a pang of guilt she responded. She apologised for not letting her know where she was and said she was safe and would like to meet her tomorrow if possible.

There was another which had come in later from Judy asking if she had heard from Jacob as he was still missing and yet another later still. Had she and Jane really been talking for so long?

She scrolled back to the first message and clicked delete. He was out there, in the ether yes, but also in the flesh. His bright eyes and his soft lips and his hands with their long sensitive fingers. The boy that she had adored.

She wondered where he was, perhaps sitting on a park bench alone in the darkness, puzzled and confused. Then again maybe he was in a pub or a café or on the train travelling away from her. Perversely she wished that she had read the text, but it was too late. The phone vibrated as another message popped onto the scrolling bar on the top of the screen.

> *You are all around me. I can smell your perfume. I can see your things. I can feel you near me.*

She gasped and although she knew it was ridiculous, she turned on the overhead light and peered around the room. Of course he wasn't there. He couldn't see her things, couldn't feel her near. Unless. And then she knew just where he was, it was obvious. He had gone to where he thought he would find her. He was at her house.

She slid from the bed and pulled on her clothes. Grabbing her keys and the mobile she crossed the room and the narrow landing. She tapped urgently on Jane's door. It opened almost immediately, and her friend stood in front of her in her pyjamas.

"What is it, is something wrong?"

Mary held out the phone and clicked the button to light the text message.

"He's at my house. I'm sure he is."

"Call the police, call them now." Her friend pushed the mobile back into Mary's hand. "Now, do it, dial 999."

"I can't."

"Don't be silly, of course you can."

"No, I can't, don't you see? If I do then all of this has been for nothing. If I call them and he's there what will they do? They'll perhaps arrest him for breaking and entering, and then what? Then I'm back into the situation I was in before. I'll have to tell them about him, about us and it's all going to come out. My mum and dad will hear about it, I'll have to go to court. They'll find out about Chloe and I promised her that wouldn't happen. I thought I was being so clever but look, I have just painted myself into a corner. I'll never be free of him, never. Unless I go now and have it out with him."

"Don't be ridiculous, what are you thinking?"

"Come with me, Jane. If there are two of us, then we'll be safe. Come with me now and I'll make him see that his best option is to go away and leave me alone. I'll tell him that if he doesn't, I'll go to the police."

"And will you?"

"Oh, I…"

"If you promise me that you will go to the police if he causes any trouble at all, then I'll come with you now and let you give him this one last chance that he doesn't deserve."

At Mary's small nod Jane turned and scooped up her clothes from the bedroom chair.

They drove in silence through the deserted streets. The phone was a mute companion though Mary held it on her lap the whole way.

Once on the driveway in front of the dark house, they sat for a while with just the click of the cooling engine disturbing the quiet.

"No sign of life." Jane was the first to speak and all Mary could do in return was shake her head. "Maybe you were wrong. Maybe he's somewhere else. Is there somewhere else?"

"No, he's here. I know he is."

They climbed from the car and by instinct they closed the doors quietly, two small thuds and then the soft pad of their shoes on the pathway. The keys slid smoothly into the newly fitted locks and Mary raised a hand and pushed the painted wood. As she did, she was swept with the memory of balloons and roses, of wine and laughter and of all the precious hopes that had crumbled and brought her to this moment.

She felt for the switch in the darkness and flicked on the wall lights. They glanced into the dim living room as they passed on the way to the kitchen. The room was as neat and clean as she had left it, and as she moved towards the window to glance into the garden Mary reached out and slid the big knife from the block. She heard Jane draw in a breath.

"He's not here, Mary."

"He is. I can feel him."

They joined hands and turned to the staircase climbing slowly.

"If he's here, why is the place in darkness?"

"I don't know, Jane, but he's here." And then she knew. She held out a hand to stop her friend. "Candles, can you smell them? He's lit candles. He's done it before."

"Your room then?"

Mary peered at the floor and pointed to where a faint flickering light at the edge of the door frame proved her correct.

"Will you wait here?" She felt rather than saw Jane shake her head.

"No bloody way. You are not going in there on your own."

Mary reached her shaking hand towards the door-knob, turning and pushing at the same time. The room was thick with perfume from the tea lights and candles that were on every surface. They saw him clearly on the bed, he was naked with just the sheet pulled to his waist. He was propped against the headboard and held a flute of sparkling wine.

Jane stood by the door, a little afraid, and a little embarrassed.

"Jacob."

"I knew you'd come." Then he leaned a little to the side. "Why is she here?"

"She's come to make sure I'm safe."

"Safe, safe from what, from whom?"

He flipped back the cover now and slid to the edge of the bed. Jane cast her gaze downward but Mary held hers on his eyes, shining in the candlelight.

"Safe from you, Jacob, to make sure you don't hurt me."

"And why would you think I would do that?"

"You did it before."

At this he gave a little toss of his head, dismissing the past.

"Well no one would blame me if I did now, after what you've done. It was you and that bitch Judy, she always had it in for me. Just another woman who needs a lesson. Anyway, I didn't come here to hurt you. I came to sort it all out. This has got completely out of hand and there is no need for it. We can put it behind us and go on. Okay, I admit that maybe I went a bit too far, I'll give you that, and I'm sorry about it but look, let's just move past it – yeah? You can publish a retraction, say it was a joke that got out of hand – something."

Mary felt Jane tense beside her.

"No, Jacob, we can't move on. We can't get past it and you can apologise, but that won't make things any better. You're sick. You need help."

"Sick, for God's sake listen to yourself. Sick. That's the trouble with you lot today," he said as he waved a hand in their direction. "You just don't understand the way things should be."

"Jacob, I'm not going to argue with you, I'm not going to forgive you and it's not my job to make you see that what you did is wrong. I just want you to go away. Get right away from here and I'll leave it at that. If you won't go, then I'm calling the police and I'm putting it all in their hands. The photographs and everything, I'll go to court and I'll see you in jail for what you did to me."

He laughed then and stood before her.

"No, no you won't, don't be ridiculous." He stepped forward and she raised her hand holding the knife.

"What the hell is that, what do you think you are doing with that?"

She heard Jane click on her phone and the ping ping as she began to dial. He lunged past her towards her friend knocking the mobile to the floor and Mary reacted without thought, grabbing at him and raising the knife to his face.

"Leave her alone, don't touch her."

He spun now and grasped her wrist in his, twisting until she screamed with the burn of it and the blade dropped from her hand. Now he had her, one arm across her chest the other round her stomach, lifting her bodily to fling her towards the bed. He threw himself across her and though she clawed and twisted he had her pinned against the mattress.

The flash took them both by surprise and they turned to where Jane stood with the phone retrieved from the floor. She was taking snap after snap of them and in her other hand was the knife held before her like a rapier. She was screaming now.

"Get off her, just get off her, or I swear I'll kill you."

He spun away from the bed and Mary launched herself after him, clinging to his waist and he stumbled and as he fell to the floor, she leapt on top of him. Jane joined her and they both sat across his back. She leaned towards him and held the knife at his face, the point against his skin.

"I have it all on my phone asshole. All recorded and it's up to you what happens to it."

He tried to speak but she dug the knife a little deeper, a drop of blood coloured the pale skin of his cheek.

"Now, just listen. You are going to get up, you are going to get dressed and then you are getting out of here. You are leaving tonight. I don't give a shit where you go but you are going now, and you are never coming back. If you come near my friend again, near this town again, then these pictures are going straight to the authorities, and not only that, they are going to the newspapers, the television. They are going on Facebook and Twitter. They are going to go so bloody viral that you won't be able to go anywhere. Everyone will know you for the woman-beating coward that you are. I don't care about your past. Your history is of no interest to me. You are a pig, and a bully. Now, do you understand me?"

She poked again at his face, he moved against the carpet and they heard him whisper.

"Pass his clothes, Mary."

As he dressed, Jane stood behind him, the knife close to him poking at him when he paused. They could tell though that the fight had gone, whether it was the shock or the threat of exposure, it didn't matter, he did as Jane told him to.

At the front door he paused and looked back at Mary standing on the bottom of the stairs, her arms wrapped protectively around her chest. He opened his mouth, drew in a breath but before he had the chance to speak Jane moved forward, still with the knife held now at arm's length.

He turned and walked away, down the path and then right and towards the main road.

Chapter 71

They locked the house and drove away.

"I don't know what to say to you, Jane. I don't know how to thank you."

Jane shook her head.

"I can't, I can't talk. I never knew I had that in me, that violence. I never thought I could feel such hate. It's scared me."

"I'm sorry."

"No, no it's not your fault – none of it is your fault."

"It feels like my fault, you could have been hurt. We both could have been, and you tried to tell me, didn't you? You tried to tell me that day in the café and I was so blind, stupid and flattered."

"Mary, you were being human, that's all. You were looking for love and we all have the right to do that."

"I can never repay what you've done tonight, you know that don't you?"

"There's no need, we're friends, we've always been friends. I'm so glad everything's okay with us now, but I do feel bad, you know, about my reaction. I cried and cried about it. I was a real bitch. Then I called your mum and I shouldn't have done, but I was worried about you. I am so sorry; I don't get any satisfaction, you know, out of what happened. I did come to see you once to tell you I was sorry but I don't think you were in."

Now was not the moment to admit that she had watched from the window as Jane had walked away.

"Can I stay tonight? Just tonight and then tomorrow well I'll think about that in the morning."

"Of course you can."

"I do need to go and meet Judy though and I think I have to tell her what happened. Why don't you come as well? You'd like her."

"Okay, yeah, I think that would be good."

The sun warmed the bright kitchen as they sat together drinking coffee. They hadn't slept but now it was morning and time to move. They didn't speak, didn't relive the events of the night before; it was too awful to discuss, and so they listened to the birds and the children in the road and they struggled with their thoughts.

They heard the car, the engine rumbled outside in the road, and there was the sound of doors slamming. It wasn't a busy street but there was no reason to assume that the noises were anything to do with them, not until the doorbell chimed.

Jane waved a hand at Mary, *stay there, I'll go*. She strode through the lounge and into the little square hallway. Through the glass of the front door she could make out two figures. A frown creased the skin of her forehead as she leaned forward and put the safety chain into the slider.

She opened the door, just a crack and the two tall figures turned to peer at her and then raised their hands to show their warrant cards. Jane's heart leapt into her mouth. Had something happened to Millie? Was her daughter was hurt? With quivering hands she slipped the chain and pulled open the door.

"What's happened, is it Millie, what's wrong?" The words tumbled over her tongue in panic, her heart was pounding her throat dry.

The taller of the two smiled at her but his eyes were wary, he had done this job before and knew just how easily things could slip out of control.

"Sorry to bother you madam, but we are looking for Mary Roland."

"Oh, thank God."

For just a moment relief wiped out everything else but then reality kicked back in.

"Are you Mary Roland, madam, or is she here? We have been told that maybe she is staying here."

Mary had heard the voices and left the kitchen. Standing in the hallway behind Jane her heart chattered and jumped. There was something wrong. The police were here, looking for her, how did they know she was here, only Judy knew?

"I'm Mary, Mary Roland. What's happened?"

"A friend, Judy Allbright gave us this address. We need to ask you a couple of questions. Are you acquainted with Jacob Chadwick madam, a student at the college?"

"Yes." Her mind was racing now and the one word was all she could manage.

"Do you mind if we come inside? We need to speak to you."

Jane opened the door and ushered them through into the living room. They took off their hats and then the taller one spoke again.

"It might be better, Ms Roland, if you sat down. We have some rather upsetting news for you."

She didn't need a second telling, all the strength had gone from her legs, she and Jane reached to each other and sat side by side hands entwined, waiting.

Chapter 72

Jane and Judy went with her. They stood in silence. They held hands as the wind whipped at their coats and lifted their hair. The weather had changed now, and the balm of summer seemed to have fled. Mary was glad of the blustery disturbance; she could blame her tears on blown grit, just the weather.

Jane hadn't known him and so had no need to grieve. Judy had known the worst of him and so had no tears to shed for his damaged soul. Mary though had seen the best of him, and it was the best of him that caused the ache in her heart and the moisture in her eyes as the vicar droned on about time and misery and dust.

There was to be an inquest of course, but at least they had been allowed to lay his body to rest. As she peered into the hole in the damp earth Mary shuddered. Bill had been cremated. The thought of Jacob's beautiful young body lying in the ground slowly disintegrating was ghastly.

She peered from under her brows at the family who stood at the other side of the grave. His mother, dry eyed but pale and hollow-looking, his brother who seemed impatient and uncomfortable. There was no one who she could identify as a father and no sister. It was a surprisingly small turnout for a young person and again this made her sad.

They didn't know where he had got the drugs, but together with the alcohol there had been little chance that he could have been saved even if they had found him sooner. He had lain on the bench in the park until mid-morning, when a dog walker had noticed that he hadn't moved since she had first seen him almost an hour before. And so they came and took him away and they had searched her out and told her because friends had said he lived with her.

"He was my lodger for just a little while. That's all." And they accepted that as fact. After all, she was old enough to be his mother, wasn't she?

Mary had stayed with Jane and together they visited the funeral directors. He looked peaceful. The way out that he had chosen hadn't disfigured his fine face. She had reached and pushed back the heavy fringe while trying to focus on the positives, to let go of the horror and to hold back the tears.

The days following his suicide were a blur. She knew that she could never go back to the house again. Her mum and dad were surprisingly supportive and bit back the questions they longed to ask, and so the small room of her childhood and youth welcomed her back and simplified her life for just a while.

It was time to change and to grow, she saw that and signed up for a course to train as a counsellor. She would take what she had learned and try to help others.

The clergyman's droning voice wound down to the dreadful end. They moved to take a turn to toss flowers and earth onto his coffin. Finally, as the small gathering dispersed, she walked with her friends down the tree lined path and left the splendour and the catastrophe that had been Jacob behind them in the cold ground.

The End

If you enjoyed this book, please let others know by leaving
a quick review on Amazon. Also, if you spot anything
untoward in the paperback, get in touch. We strive for the
best quality and appreciate reader feedback.

editor@thebookfolks.com

www.thebookfolks.com

Other books by Diane Dickson:

BLURRED LINES
BRAZEN ESCAPE
BRUTAL PURSUIT
BURNING GREED
BROKEN ANGEL

BODY ON THE SHORE
BODY BY THE DOCKS
BODY OUT OF PLACE
BODY IN THE SQUAT
BODY IN THE CANAL
BODY ON THE ESTATE
BODY BELOW THE BRIDGE
BODY IN THE WAY

TWIST OF TRUTH
TANGLED TRUTH
BONE BABY
LEAVING GEORGE
WHO FOLLOWS
THE GRAVE
LAYERS OF LIES
DEPTHS OF DECEPTION
YOU'RE DEAD
SINGLE TO EDINBURGH
HOPELESS